"What about y... ... *you gotten to the altar?"*

"How close? Actually, I prefer to stay as far away as I can manage."

"Ah." Zack nodded. "Sounds like someone broke your heart, too."

"No. No broken heart. I just don't figure myself the sort cut out for matrimony."

His eyebrows shot up in surprise. "Hmm. Can't say I've ever met a woman who shared your view."

"Well, I am one of a kind."

"Yes, Jaye," he said slowly. "I'm coming to realize that."

Dear Reader,

I started writing romance novels for the same reason I began reading them when I was a teenager. I love *love*. In real life, stories about how people met their spouses fascinate me. Sometimes I'm truly amazed that two people manage to find each other, fall in love and then overcome all of the obstacles life throws their way.

I'm also a huge fan of happy endings. I like knowing that I'm going to feel upbeat when I finish a book. As we all know, life doesn't always hand us a satisfying conclusion. I can recall some pretty low points in my life when reading a good romance novel provided a much needed escape from reality.

I hope you enjoy Zack and Jaye's story in *Moonlight and Roses*.

Best wishes,

Jackie Braun

JACKIE BRAUN

Moonlight and Roses

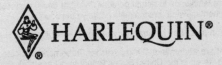

HARLEQUIN®

TORONTO • NEW YORK • LONDON
AMSTERDAM • PARIS • SYDNEY • HAMBURG
STOCKHOLM • ATHENS • TOKYO • MILAN • MADRID
PRAGUE • WARSAW • BUDAPEST • AUCKLAND

ISBN-13: 978-0-373-17491-1
ISBN-10:   0-373-17491-8

MOONLIGHT AND ROSES

First North American Publication 2008.

www.eHarlequin.com

Printed in U.S.A.

Jackie Braun worked as an award-winning editorial writer before leaving her job at a daily newspaper to write romance. She is a two-time RITA® Award finalist, a three-time National Readers' Choice Award finalist and a past winner of the Rising Star Award in traditional romance. She lives in Michigan with her husband and son, and can be reached through her Web site, www.jackiebraun.com.

"I enjoy wine—the drier the better—but before writing this book I had no idea of the work that goes into producing a quality product. Winemaking is as much an art as it is a science. I raise my glass to the world's vintners, artists all."
—Jackie Braun on *Moonlight and Roses*

Look out for Jackie's next book

EXPECTING A MIRACLE

Out in April, only from Harlequin Romance®.

For my good friend, Tina Haas, who didn't complain one bit when I asked her to help me research a winery in Leelanau County. And to the staff at Black Star Farms, who made our stay there an incredible experience. Any errors I made or liberties I took in writing this book bear no reflection on their winemaking knowledge and skill.

PROLOGUE

JAYE MONROE didn't consider herself the sort of woman to swoon, but as she sat with her stepmother in the stuffy office, listening to the lawyer read the contents of Frank Monroe's will, she definitely felt light-headed.

Not only was her beloved father gone, but he'd left their Leelanau County vineyard, along with its winery and tasting room, in the sole possession of his second wife of seven years rather the daughter who had toiled by his side for the past nine to help make the Medallion label an up-and-coming success.

Upon hearing this, Margaret sent Jaye a spiteful grin, but the older woman's glee didn't last long.

The lawyer was saying, "As for the house, the collection of original eighteenth-century artwork and all of the antique furnishings with the exception of those found in the master bedroom suite, Frank wanted you to have those, Jaye."

"What?" both women shouted simultaneously.

Jaye straightened in her seat. Her stepmother slumped sideways.

"Mrs. Monroe?" the lawyer said, rising partway from his chair. "Are you all right?"

Jaye knew Margaret wasn't the sort to swoon, either, but the older woman certainly enjoyed attention and had a flair for the dramatic.

"Water," Margaret murmured, her heavily made-up eyelids flickering. "I need water."

"What about you, Miss Monroe?" the lawyer asked. "Can I get you anything?"

Jaye considered requesting a shot of something potent to numb the pain and outrage she was experiencing, but she shook her head.

When he returned, she said in as steady a voice as she could manage, "This can't be right, Mr. Danielson. You must have read that part backward. Dad wouldn't leave the vineyard to Margaret. She doesn't want it any more than I want a house filled with old paintings and gaudy antiques."

"I paid good money for those old paintings and gaudy antiques," Margaret snapped, apparently having recovered from her near collapse.

"Yes, you enjoyed spending *my* father's money on anything that caught your eye."

"He was *my* husband, so it was *my* money to spend," the older woman retorted. Then she slumped back in her seat again. "I loved that man. What will I do without him?"

"Ladies, please." Jonas Danielson raised a bony hand to silence them. "I'm sorry, Miss Monroe, Mrs. Monroe.

I know this must come as a shock to both of you, but this is what Frank stipulated in the will he had drawn up just prior to his death last month."

"It doesn't make any sense," Jaye persisted. "I have my own house, my own furniture." All of which leaned toward the contemporary. "Dad and I built Medallion together. He can't have intended to pull the rug out from under me this way."

Mr. Danielson retrieved a couple of papers from a folder and handed one to Jaye and one to Margaret. "Perhaps this will help clarify the matter for you."

It was the photocopy of a letter. Jaye recognized her father's scratchy cursive immediately, and her heart began to race. The letter began: "Dear Margaret and Juliet."

Juliet. Her father only used Jaye's given name when she was in trouble, and boy was she ever, she realized, as she continued to read the words he'd penned.

I know that the two of you have never been close, which is a pity since neither of you really has anyone else. I want the two women I love the most in this world to look after each other and to work together after I'm gone. I think this is a good way to ensure that you will.

Juliet, Margaret will need help with Medallion's daily operations. Margaret, I know you've never taken an interest in the vineyard, but you are a bright and capable woman. I think you will be an asset. In the meantime, I'm sure Juliet will allow you to reside in the house as always, and I ask that you allow Juliet to continue as head vintner at the winery. There's no one I trust more to ensure the label's quality and success.

I love you both and it saddens me to leave you. My only comfort is in knowing that you will have each other to lean on. Please, be good to each other.

Jaye traced his signature at the bottom of the page and then glanced over at Margaret, who was still busy reading, if the movement of her lips was any indication.

Be good to each other.

Jaye bit the inside of her cheek to keep from laughing. He might as well have asked them to flap their arms and fly. The two women had never been friends. Oh, they could manage to be cordial when the circumstances required it. On holidays, for instance, they sat together at the dinner table and exchanged polite small talk. But when it came right down to it, Jaye found the older woman vacuous and self-centered. Margaret was no fonder of Jaye, whom she'd often labeled as outspoken and a tomboy.

No, the women were not friends. They had tolerated each other for Frank's sake. Now that he was gone so was all pretense, as Margaret's next words made clear.

"I'm hiring my own lawyer. This is ridiculous." She stood, crumpled up the letter and tossed it onto the lawyer's desk. "*Everything* should be mine! I'm sure a judge will agree. I was his wife."

"Of seven years." Jaye stood as well. "I'm his daughter of nearly thirty. Yes, I can see how giving you everything, even the vineyard that you've never stepped foot in, would be fair."

Margaret's eyes narrowed. "He loved me. That still kills you, doesn't it?"

Jaye ignored the question, partly because it was true. Of all the women in the world for her father to marry, why did it have to be a silly bit of arm candy like Margaret?

"I'll hire a lawyer, too," she vowed. "We'll see who ends up with what."

"Ladies, ladies," Mr. Danielson pleaded. "Are you sure that's what you want to do? Litigation could take months, years. It will be draining emotionally, not to mention financially. Why not compromise? The solution in this matter seems obvious. If you don't want the vineyard," he said to Margaret, "and you don't want the house and its furnishings," his gaze moved to Jaye, "then perhaps you can make arrangements to transfer ownership?"

"That sounds reasonable," Jaye allowed.

But Margaret was shaking her head, her expression far more shrewd than vacuous now. "I don't know," she said slowly. "All of that acreage would fetch a pretty price in this real estate market, especially without a bunch of damned grapes growing on it."

Jaye knew a moment of true horror. She wouldn't put it past her stepmother to sell the vineyard's prime property to the highest bidder. "I'll give you everything my father left me, plus a fair sum."

"Will you now?" Margaret's smile bloomed.

"Yes. This was Dad's dream, Margaret. The vineyard represents all of his years of hard work." And mine, Jaye thought. And mine. "Promise me that you won't sell Medallion to a developer."

Margaret studied Jaye for a long moment before finally nodding. Still, Jaye didn't quite trust the gleam in her eye. "Okay, Jaye. You're right. This was Frank's dream. So, I promise you that I won't sell it to a developer."

And she didn't. Five months later, after Jaye had accepted an offer for her beachfront home and was busily scraping together the rest of the down payment for the vineyard, Margaret sold the Medallion Winery to a California vintner.

CHAPTER ONE

JAYE stood on the upstairs balcony of the house her father had left to her and watched the silver convertible shoot up the paved road that led to Medallion's winery, tasting room and business offices. She caught a glimpse of sandy hair, ruddy cheeks and a cocky smile. The car's top was down despite the fact that the outside temperature was flirting with fifty.

If it were later in the day, she might wonder if the fool driving had already imbibed a bit too freely at one of the area's many other wineries. Since it was just past eight in the morning she doubted that was the case. Besides, she figured she knew exactly who was driving that fancy foreign number.

Zackary Holland.

Even thinking his name had her lip curling. The man had pulled up stakes at his family's century-old Napa Valley vineyard and bought Medallion from Margaret before Jaye even had known a deal was in the works.

Jaye hadn't met Zack yet, although it looked like she

was going to have the privilege today. She wasn't looking forward to it, even if she was anxious to get it over with and find out where things stood. Where *she* stood. She wanted Medallion back, and eventually she would have it. A man who would slough off his birthright surely could be talked into parting with this vineyard. In the meantime, she wanted to keep her job as head vintner.

Usually, Jaye wasn't one given to snap judgments, but she doubted she would find she liked Zack very much and not just because he owned what by right should have been hers. Having traveled in wine circles, she figured she knew his type. She'd met more than one pompous, pedigreed vineyard heir who considered substandard any American wine produced east of the West Coast, a couple of New England vintages excepted.

As a child, Jaye had led a comfortable life thanks to her father's keen knack for investment, but after college she'd earned her own way, putting in fifty hours or more each week at the vineyard to draw a paycheck. The Zack Hollands of the world didn't earn their way. Some of them never bothered to learn more about the making of wine than how to assess their family's finished product from pricy stemware.

She surveyed the acres of terraced grapevines that were spread out like the quaint pattern of a quilt on the surrounding hillsides. Cabernet, chardonnay, and pinot were among the varieties she'd helped her father graft and plant. In the distance beyond them, the maples and oaks were starting to change color, sprinkling the horizon with splashes of red and gold that heralded fall as surely as the crisp air that turned her breath white.

It was nearly harvest time and this year promised one of the best yields yet at Medallion. Jaye and her father had spent the past nine years toiling and sweating, first to establish the vineyard and then to earn recognition for their wines. Finally they were succeeding. She swallowed around the lump in her throat. All of that hard work, and her father hadn't lived to see the fruits of their labor.

She swiped at the tears that streaked her face, irritated to find them there. Again. She wasn't one to cry, although she'd done her fair share in recent months. She didn't like it. After all, what was the point of crying? What had railing against fate ever changed for her in the past? Her mother hadn't come back. Her father couldn't. The vineyard? Time would tell.

She returned inside, plaited her heavy hair into its usual no-nonsense braid and dressed for work. Unless—or until—the new owner told her to clear out her desk and leave, she had a job to do.

Zack parked his car and got out. Then he stood, feet planted shoulder width apart, and grinned as wide as his wind-numbed face would allow. His previous visit to the vineyard hadn't prepared him for the beauty to come. Oh, the area had been pretty in late summer with all of those shades of blue and green, but decked out in the bold hues of autumn it simply dazzled.

He'd arrived in Michigan late the evening before,

taking a suite of rooms at a hotel in nearby Traverse City. Until he found a permanent home, he would be living there. When he'd awakened this morning, he'd felt like a child on Christmas, too keyed up to choke down more than a couple bites of toast before he'd hopped in his car and followed the highway that bordered the aquamarine waters of Traverse Bay. Halfway to the vineyard, he'd stopped to put down the top on his Mercedes. He'd wanted an unrestricted view of his surroundings.

He rubbed his stiff fingers before stuffing his hands into the pockets of his jeans. He was paying for his impulsiveness now, but he didn't care. He felt more alive than he had in years. Anticipation hummed inside him as he entered the tasting room at Medallion. This winery was his and his alone. He would set its course, decide its future, and call all of the shots. He wouldn't have to run his ideas past anyone else for approval that ultimately would be denied. No. He was in charge.

He revised his opinion half an hour later when a woman stalked through the main doors of the tasting room. He pegged her age at about thirty and her mood as supremely agitated if the stiff set of her shoulders and grim line of her mouth were any indication.

She was tall, only a few inches shorter than his six-foot-two, and lean. What he could see of her figure beneath a bulky wool sweater and loose-fitting carpenter jeans might best be described as willowy. She certainly commanded attention, though. The workers stopped what they were doing, glancing around nervously. An unnatural silence fell, and even though no one moved, Zack got the distinct impression sides had been taken.

Hers had more.

"You must be Juliet Monroe." No introduction was necessary, but he made one anyway. He believed in confronting awkwardness head-on. And so he extended a hand as he crossed to where she stood. "I've heard a lot about you. I'm Zack Holland."

Up close he realized her eyes were green and that the hair she'd scraped back into an unflattering braid was the color of freshly ground cinnamon. Something about her tugged at him, although he couldn't figure out why. She wasn't beautiful, at least not in the classical sense, or even in the chic sense like his former fiancée, Mira, who had turned heads wherever they'd gone.

Given Jaye's prominent cheekbones, slightly flared nose and wide-set eyes, the best word to describe her would be *striking*.

Her mouth was on the broad side, too, and her lips might have been full, although at the moment it was hard to tell as they were compressed into a frown. They loosened slightly, but only so she could tell him, "I don't care to be called Juliet."

Zack managed to keep his smile in place despite her clipped tone. This meeting had to be difficult for her, and he didn't mind letting her save face in front of the workers—as long as it didn't come at his expense. Everyone needed to understand and accept that he was in charge now, Juliet Monroe perhaps most of all.

"What *do* you care to be called?"

"Jaye. I go by Jaye." Her grip was firm to the point of being painful when she finally shook his hand. He half expected her to challenge him to a thumb war.

"Jaye." He nodded once. The short, boyish name fit her, since there was little about her that seemed soft or overtly feminine, except maybe the long hair. What would it look like...? He tamped down his curiosity. "It's nice to meet you."

She nodded but didn't actually return the sentiment. Instead she got right down to business. "I'd like to know what your plans are for Medallion." She spread her hand out to encompass the room's wide-eyed occupants. "And for its workers, of course."

Around them people shuffled their feet and murmured. Zack cleared his throat. He hadn't expected to be put on the spot. Nor was he used to being challenged by an employee.

"I'm going to hold a staff meeting at the end of the week to go over the particulars, once I've had a good look around. I have some changes in mind," he said, being purposefully vague.

"Such as?"

The woman was tenacious; he'd give her that. Under other circumstances, he might have admired the quality. At the moment, though, he found it insolent and annoying.

"They'll keep. But if you've got a minute, I'd like to talk to you."

He was well aware that everyone was watching

them and cataloging Zack and Jaye's every word, glance and gesture.

"I'm at your disposal," she drawled.

Right, he thought. When she made no effort to move, he added, "Why don't we go to my office?"

Jaye let Zack lead the way, even though she knew every step by heart. The business offices were located up a flight of stairs just off the tasting room. The biggest one was at the end of the hall. It made sense that it would be the one he'd claim as his own. Still, when the door closed behind them, Jaye felt her heart squeeze. The office, with its grand, panoramic view of the vineyard, had been her father's.

Nothing of Frank Monroe's belongings remained. She'd cleared out every last note card and paperclip after her stepmother announced the vineyard's sale. But she could still feel him here. She could smell the tangy tobacco he'd smoked in his pipe, and it took no effort at all to envision his bulky frame sitting behind a cluttered desk wearing his usual uniform of wrinkled khaki trousers, a Greek fisherman's cap and a navy button-down shirt, the breast pocket of which bulged from his glasses case and assorted other personal effects. Jaye swore her father carried more things in his pockets than most women did in their purses.

"Everything okay?" Zack asked.

The image dissolved. She glanced over to find Medallion's new owner standing beside her. She'd forgotten all about him for a moment as she'd stared at the empty desk and remembered...mourned. Her father had been gone nearly six months, but the ache had not lessened. If anything, it seemed to grow worse as the reality of never seeing him again set in and festered like an infected sore.

She felt too raw, too exposed, to answer Zack's question, so she asked one of her own. "What did you want to see me about?"

Zack leaned one hip on the edge of the desk. "I thought that would be obvious."

She swallowed as a lead weight settled in her stomach. "You're letting me go."

"No," he said slowly, hardly sounding decisive.

Jaye crossed her arms. "You mean, not yet."

He ran a hand over the back of his neck and chuckled, but he sounded more frustrated than amused when he said, "You don't like to make things easy, do you?"

She'd lost her father, their vineyard, and now her livelihood was on the line. "In my experience, nothing worth having comes easily."

She meant Medallion, recalling the backbreaking hours she and her father had spent grafting vines to root stock, fixing trellises, warding off pests and praying for just the right mix of sunshine and rain to produce a good crop.

To her surprise, Zack nodded, as if he understood completely. But what could have been difficult for Mr. Silver Spoon to attain?

"I'd appreciate your cooperation, Jaye. This transition is difficult for everyone, perhaps you most of all, but it won't become any easier if Medallion's workers feel they have to choose between us."

"I'm not asking them to choose."

"No?" His brows rose.

"I care about them," she insisted. "They're good workers, good people. They have families to feed. I don't want to see them strung along."

"I won't string anyone along. But I didn't appreciate being put on the spot down there." He waved a hand in the direction of the door.

"I'm sorry." She tried to sound sincere, but she couldn't resist adding, "If you felt that's what I was doing."

Zack inhaled deeply, but apparently decided to drop the matter because he changed the subject. "I'm impressed with the operation here. It's well run, and the finished product shows incredible potential. I understand from the workers that you're largely responsible for making this a first-class facility."

She wasn't comfortable with the compliment. "I played a small role. It was my father's doing. He loved Medallion and liked nothing better than seeing it succeed against bigger and supposedly better wineries both here and around the world."

"I'm sorry for your loss. I understand that he died this past spring."

"Yes." The pain of hearing those words still surprised her, but she managed a polite nod. "Thank you."

"I met your father once."

This news had her full attention. "You did? When was that?"

"A few years back at a wine competition in San

Diego. It must have been the first year Medallion entered. Your chardonnay did well as I recall."

Jaye wrinkled her nose. "Honorable mention. I thought it had a shot at silver. Bronze at the very least."

"It was pretty good," he said, as if he really remembered.

"Holland Farms took the gold."

"Yes." She thought he might gloat over his family's win, but he didn't. Instead he said, "I liked your father. We had dinner one night. Frank Monroe listened to some ideas I had." His expression turned thoughtful. "He was a really good listener."

Her throat ached too much to speak, so she merely nodded. She and her father had spent many afternoons in this very room, talking, and not all of their conversations had centered on wine.

"I don't recall seeing you there," Zack said.

"San Diego?"

"Uh-huh."

Jaye wasn't one to get dolled up, let alone mix and mingle. She was more comfortable in casual pants and loafers than in cocktail dresses and high heels. What's more she'd never understood the point of making small talk with strangers or chatting about the weather— unless, of course, the local forecast was calling for something that might harm the grapes.

Frank Monroe had often bemoaned the fact that he'd turned his only daughter into a tomboy, so much so that as an adult she was more interested in grafting vines than going out on dates. But Jaye had no regrets. Oh, she liked men and she did date, ending things amiably when her suitors turned serious. She wasn't commitmentphobic, as her best friend, Corey Worth, claimed. Jaye just didn't see the point in settling down and starting a family. To her way of thinking, it was better to know now that she wasn't the wife and mother type than to do what her mom had done: marry, have a child and then take off for parts unknown with nary a look back.

"I'm not a very memorable person," she told Zack.

He surprised her by replying, "I don't know about that. You make quite an impression."

His gaze was direct and it made her oddly uncomfortable. For the first time in memory, Jaye felt self-conscious and wished she'd taken a little more care with her appearance. What exactly she would have done differently, she wasn't sure. She only knew that compared to Zack, who stood before her in tailored trousers and a designer shirt that screamed expensive, she felt drab and outdated.

She noticed other things about him then. What filled out his clothes wasn't bad, either. He had broad shoulders, long limbs and narrow hips. He appeared fit, as if he might work out regularly. But he wasn't overly muscled.

While his body was definitely a prime specimen, it was his face that could make a woman forget her name. Paul Newman–blue eyes peaked out from beneath a slash of brows that were a good two shades darker than the sandy hair on his head. The hair had a nice wave to it, the kind women paid big money to achieve. And he wore it longer than most professional men did. Not quite long enough to pull into a ponytail, but it brushed his shirt's collar in the back and gave him a slightly dangerous look that was in stark contrast to his otherwise tidy appearance.

Jaye resisted the urge to fiddle with the end of her braid. "Actually, I didn't go with my dad that time. I stayed behind to look after things at the vineyard."

"That explains it then," Zack said. "I never forget a face."

"I never forget a wine. Your chardonnay was exceptional that year." It was a relief to return to the subject of grapes. She always felt on firm footing when the discussion centered on business.

"Yes, Holland's was," he said. Again, he seemed to distance himself from taking any credit. "I think Medallion's has the potential to be even better."

"Really?" she asked, too intrigued to act blasé.

"I wouldn't have bought this vineyard if I felt otherwise," he replied.

The reminder of the winery's change in ownership tempered her enthusiasm. "I see."

"I was disappointed I didn't get a chance to meet you when I toured Medallion before making my initial offer," Zack said.

"I was out of the country at the time."

He nodded. "A buying trip. France, I believe your mother told me."

"Margaret is my *step*mother." She snapped out the correction. "I was not informed of your visit until well after my return. In fact, I wasn't informed that the vineyard had changed hands until after the deal was done."

He blinked in surprise. "I…I didn't realize."

Jaye saw no point in beating around the bush. "Medallion should have been mine."

"But your father didn't leave it to you."

His equally blunt statement had her bristling. "Dad thought he could micromanage a peace treaty between his second wife and me from the grave. He was wrong."

"I'm sorry."

"I don't want your pity," she replied.

"Actually, that was an expression of sympathy," he said, making her feel small.

Jaye paced to the window in an effort to regroup. Her anger, justified as it was, was of no use here. So she moderated her tone and said evenly, "I want the vineyard, Mr. Holland. I'm prepared to offer you what you paid plus a little something extra for your trouble."

"Why don't you call me Zack? And it looks like we have a problem." He joined her at the window. "I want Medallion, too. I'm not interested in selling."

His reply was nothing less than Jaye had expected. After all, she had made the same offer to Margaret without success. Yet the disappointment of hearing him say the words nearly leveled her.

"Is that going to be an issue for you?" he asked.

She swallowed her outrage along with a good helping of pride. "I don't have much choice but to accept that you'll be the one calling the shots from now on."

To her surprise, he laughed out loud. "Gee, that sounds convincing."

"I said I would *accept* it. I didn't say anything about liking it."

"Ah. Thanks for the clarification."

While Zack appeared amused, Jaye was dead serious when she said, "I'm very good at my job. I…I would appreciate it if you would allow me to stay on."

He nodded. "I'd like that. You know the local people, not to mention the regional quirks of the Great Lakes growing season, far better than I do at this point. I'd like you to manage things."

"But I'm the head vintner. Tom Worley manages Medallion's operation."

"Not anymore. He'll be reassigned or offered a compensation package. Think you can handle it?"

She bristled at his tone. "There's not a job at Medallion I haven't done at one time or another. My father thought it was important to know the business inside and out. He didn't believe you could be an effective leader without understanding the jobs of the people you were leading."

"Is that a subtle barb?" he asked.

"Of course not." Before she could censor the thought, she added, "I wasn't trying to be subtle."

She expected him to be annoyed, perhaps angry. Instead he laughed.

"Do you think I've never worked a harvest or shoveled grapes into a crusher?"

"Have you?" Jaye asked.

"Yes. But I don't think I have to work every job to understand its demands or to appreciate the people I pay to perform it."

"Fair enough. So, if I'm no longer head vintner, who'll be in charge of winemaking?" she asked.

Zack only smiled.

"You?" Her tone was incredulous, so much so it bordered on insulting.

"No need to look so shocked. I have some prior experience," he informed her.

Jaye wasn't impressed by his claim. All she could see was that she would have her hands full in the coming months, likely pulling double duty while he dabbled. She cleared her throat. "I believe in being honest."

"That's good to know," he said slowly.

"I'll stay on, managing and assisting with the winemaking when necessary—"

"You're already assuming I'll need your help?"

"I said I believe in being honest."

"Yes, but what about tactful?" he asked wryly.

"I'll work on it."

"Fair enough," he replied.

"As I said, I'll stay on, but I won't be doing it for you or even for the paycheck."

His eyes narrowed. "Go on."

"I've got an investment here that goes well beyond money. Your name might be on the deed now, but make no mistake, Mr. Holland—"

"Zack," he said, for the first time sounding truly annoyed. "My name is Zack."

"Fine. Zack. I want Medallion. And I plan to keep making you fair offers for its sale until you finally accept one. I don't give up easily."

"So I've noticed." Then his expression turned oddly grim. "Do you love it that much?"

"Love it?" Jaye shook her head, not surprised in the least that someone who could walk away from his family's land would fail to understand the attachment she had to hers. "This vineyard is everything to me."

"Everything? It's just a place. It's not…people."

"No. It's more reliable than people." She hadn't meant to say that. Thankfully, he didn't understand her meaning.

"It's dirt and vines. It's real estate, an investment," he countered, blue eyes glittering like ice.

"Is that all it is to you?"

Zack didn't say anything, although for a moment she thought she saw something contradictory flicker in his expression. Then it was gone.

"Well, that's not all it is to me." She glanced back out the window. Her voice was low, her tone reverent when she added, "My dad and I built Medallion from nothing. It's…it's my life."

CHAPTER TWO

ZACK spent the following week getting acquainted with the winery's day-to-day operations and the people who performed them. As he'd told Jaye on the first day, other than the manager and the vintner, he didn't have any immediate plans to let people go, change their duties or make new hires, but neither did he intend to maintain the status quo. He saw potential at Medallion for greater profit, just as he saw potential for a superior product. He planned to achieve both.

Zack had something to prove.

He was sitting at his desk late Friday going through invoices when the telephone rang. It was his mother.

"I thought I'd call since you haven't." Judith Holland's tone held teasing censure as well as a little hurt. He regretted that. It wasn't his intention to wound her.

"Sorry. It's been a busy couple weeks. The harvest is beginning," he said.

"Here, too." It was her subtle way of saying she didn't buy his excuse.

"How is it looking?" he couldn't help asking. Hearing her voice had made him a little homesick for California and the vineyard he'd left behind. Winemaking was in his blood. It had been in the Holland blood for three generations.

"Good," she said. "Ross says it will be a better yield than last year, especially for the Sangioveses."

"That must please Dad." The Italian varietal was one of his father's personal favorites.

"It does. Phillip thinks we should expand that section of the vineyard and increase our production, given the rise in popularity of the wine."

"Of course he does." Zack's mood soured. He'd suggested the very same thing to his father two years ago without success, but only because Phillip had been against it at the time.

Phillip was Zack's cousin but the two men were more like brothers. They had been raised together after a car accident had left a four-year-old Phillip orphaned. Zack had been two at the time. Over the years the pair had butted heads often, enjoying what his mother termed sibling rivalry. It had run deeper than that. Now as adults, Holland Farms and their opposing visions for it posed the biggest source of friction.

No matter what innovations or changes Zack proposed, to make the staid winery stand out in a changing and ever more competitive marketplace, his cousin effectively vetoed them. It wasn't that Phillip had any more say or power than Zack did. No, what he had was more damning. He had Zack's father's ear. He'd *always* had his father's ear.

"How is old Phil these days?" Zack drawled. "Still sitting to the right hand of the father?"

"Zackary." Judith's tone sounded more weary than scolding.

"Sorry." And he was. He hadn't meant to put his mother in the middle.

She seemed satisfied with the apology. "Your cousin is well."

"And Mira?"

"She's well, too." The words came out slowly.

"They're still together then?" he asked.

Zack's fiancée's affections had soured quickly when he began talking about selling off his share of Holland Farms and shopping for his own vineyard. Soon after ending things with Zack, she'd turned up on Phillip's arm at his family's annual charity ball. It had been a hell of blow to his ego to learn that she'd considered the vineyard to be Zack's most appealing attribute.

"Yes." Judith cleared her throat before continuing. "In fact, she and Phillip recently became engaged."

It wasn't heartache he felt. He'd moved beyond that. What was left was bitterness. "Proof that one Holland is as good as the next as long as he comes with a stake in the land," he sneered.

"Zackary, please. It's been nearly a year. Don't be like that."

"Like what, Mother? Honest?" He snorted. "Apparently I'm the only one so afflicted in our family.

Everyone else just tiptoes around the fact that my cousin has always taken what belongs to me."

She didn't dispute that. Instead, she said, "They love one another."

"They love Holland and the lifestyle it affords them," Zack countered.

"You used to love Holland, too."

"Yes. I loved it enough to want to see it evolve." He let out a sigh. "It's not worth getting into again. Not over the phone and not with you, Mom." She'd always been in his corner. "I know you supported my ideas."

"I did and I still do. I know you'll do well." There was a hitch in her voice when she said, "I just wish Michigan weren't so far away."

"It's just a plane ride," he said lightly.

"Yes, just a plane ride," she repeated. Then, "Are you upset about Mira?"

"Not the way you think."

"Good. Mira is a nice young woman, but she wasn't right for you, Zack. You never would have been happy married to her," Judith said.

"That much we can agree on. So, when are they planning to make it official?"

"In the spring." She hesitated a moment before asking, "You'll come home for the wedding, won't you?"

"What and ruin my black sheep image?" His laughter held no humor. "Sorry, Mom. I think I'll send my regrets."

"There will always be a place for you here." Judith's voice was low, broken.

"I know that's how you feel, Mom, and I appreciate it. Really, I do." Left unsaid was that his father and cousin had long made him feel like an outsider. Mira's defection had been the final straw. There would be no going back, at least not until he'd achieved some of the ambitious goals he'd set for himself.

"Are you happy?" his mother asked quietly.

"I'm getting there." The reply wasn't only for her benefit. Zack meant it.

"That's good. I want you to be happy even more than I want you here. I love you."

"I love you, too, Mom."

After hanging up, he decided to call it a day. The sun had set already, and he was tired and not likely to get much more done—especially now. He felt too unsettled, too restless to sit behind his desk and sift through papers. His stomach rumbled noisily and he realized he was also hungry.

When he stepped out of his office, he noticed that Jaye was still in hers. Through the open door, he could see her hunched at her desk, reading a report. Her hair was in its usual utilitarian braid and she wore a flannel shirt that looked to be at least a couple of sizes too large. A bottle of spring water sat open next to her elbow, and she was munching on a granola bar.

He stopped at her door. "Please tell me that's not your dinner," he said.

Jaye glanced up at the sound of his voice and blinked as if trying to focus. In the past week Zack had learned one thing about her: she was no slacker. The woman put in long hours and gave everything she worked on her undivided attention.

"Sorry? What did you say?" she asked.

He motioned toward the bar of rolled oats and raisins she held in one hand. "I was just wondering if that was your dinner."

"Oh?" She shook her head. "A late lunch, actually."

"It's going on seven."

She glanced in the direction of the window, as if just realizing it was dark outside. "A *really* late lunch, then," she said.

He leaned against the doorjamb. "I can see how you manage to stay so slim. Got something against real food?"

"This *is* real food, but to answer your question, no. I just didn't have time to stop for a meal today."

He nodded and straightened, intending to be on his way. But he found himself saying, "I was thinking about grabbing a bite to eat before I head back to my hotel. Would you like to join me?"

Jaye eyed him the way a scientist might study an acutely contagious test subject and said nothing.

"You know, you're hell on a man's ego," Zack drawled, snorting out a laugh afterward.

"Sorry. I just…I just don't think that we should—"

"What?" He cocked one eyebrow in challenge. "Be friendly? I'm not asking you out, Jaye." Thinking of Mira and all of the pain and disillusionment she'd caused, he added with great feeling, "Believe me, I'm not interested."

"And you have the nerve to say I'm hell on the ego," she replied dryly.

He closed his eyes, rubbed them and sighed. "Sorry. That came out wrong."

"Bad day?"

Zack shook his head. "Just a long one. A long week, for that matter." Now the weekend yawned before him. More than likely he would spend it in his office. Better there than alone in a hotel room with nothing to do. "Well, I'll leave you to your late lunch. See you Monday."

He was turning to go when Jaye said, "Friday is pizza night."

He angled back. "Pardon?"

"It's Geneva's night off. She's my housekeeper. She plays bridge with her friends on Fridays, so I make pizza."

"From scratch?" He was having a hard time picturing Jaye puttering around in a kitchen. She didn't appear to be the domestic sort, given her affinity for men's shirts and steel-toed work boots.

She shrugged. "It's not like it's rocket science. Besides, I buy the dough already made from a pizzeria in Sutton's Bay. Saves me time."

"I see." He motioned with one hand. "So, are you extending an invitation to me or are you just sharing information?"

His ego took another beating when she took her time answering. "I'm extending an invitation, one coworker to another."

He decided not to point out that technically he was her boss. "Gee, glad we have that straight."

Jaye tossed the uneaten portion of her granola bar into the trash. "Give me five minutes to finish up here."

"Okay. I'll meet you downstairs."

Jaye didn't know what had possessed her to invite Zack to dinner, and at her house no less. She didn't want him in her home, invading more of her space. But there was no use wasting time regretting it now. The deed was done, and unless she planned to uninvite him, which she didn't, she was going to be spending the next couple of hours in his company.

The idea wasn't completely without appeal. She told herself that was because they had winemaking in common, which meant at the very least the conversation would be easy and interesting. Besides, what was that saying? Keep your friends close and your enemies closer. Zack wasn't her enemy exactly, but under the circumstances, neither was he her friend.

Downstairs, the tasting room had closed a couple of hours earlier and all of the employees had long since gone home. Stemmed glasses had been washed and put up, the hardwood surface of the large circular bar had been wiped down, and any opened bottles of wine properly stored. The security lights glowed softly, giving the large space with its vaulted ceiling and exposed oak beams a more intimate feel.

"Zack?" she called out.

"Over here." He stepped from behind a display of bottles that had been stacked on their sides to keep the corks moist.

"What are you doing?" she asked.

"My mom told me never to show up at someone's home empty-handed, so I'm looking for a little something to go with our dinner." He flashed an engaging grin that, along with the reference to his mother, made him appear far younger than the midthirties she knew him to be.

Jaye pointed to the next shelf over. "How about the house red?"

"It's good." He scratched his chin. "But I was thinking of something a little more…elegant."

"To go with pizza?"

Zack shrugged. "Is there a rule against that?"

"I guess not."

"Good. Besides, I feel like celebrating."

"Let me guess. Ownership of the vineyard?" Her tone was tight.

To her surprise he shook his head. "I was thinking more along the lines of freedom."

His lips twisted on the last word, as if it had left a foul taste in his mouth. Jaye didn't press him, even though the cryptic answer certainly made her curious. Freedom from what? Or the more intriguing question: Freedom from whom?

It was none of her business, though. So she asked instead, "If it's a celebration you have in mind, then how about our 2004 pinot noir?"

"Ah. Now you're talking."

He grinned again. This time there was nothing remotely boyish about the way he looked. He was all man, fully grown and way too easy on the eyes. Jaye swallowed. Friend? Enemy? For a moment her traitorous libido seemed interested in drafting an entirely different classification. She chalked it up to long work days and a virtually nonexistent social life, especially when it came to members of the opposite sex.

"I'll wait for you outside," she told him, and hastily retreated, happy to stand alone in the frigid moonlight while her pulse returned to normal.

Jaye was leaning against his car when Zack finished locking up the building's main doors. Unless she had appointments that took her away from the vineyard during the day, he'd noted that she walked the short distance from the house to work.

"Car's unlocked," he called. "I should have thought to give you the keys so you could start it up and get the heater going."

The air held an extra bite tonight, but she didn't look cold. In fact, her jacket remained unzipped.

"That's okay. I was just enjoying the peace."

"It's like this at night back home, too," he commented as he drew closer.

"Like what?"

He motioned with the bottle of wine to encompass the dark countryside beyond the lighted parking lot. "Isolated and quiet. It's easy to forget the rest of the world exists beyond the vineyard once the visitors go home for the day and the sun sets."

"My dad used to claim I did that even when it was light outside."

"A bit of a homebody?" Zack asked as he joined her on the passenger side of the car.

"I date." She sounded slightly defensive.

"I don't believe I said otherwise, Jaye." He opened her door. The basic courtesy that was so common on the dates she claimed to go on had her brows lifting. Still, she said nothing as she folded those long legs of hers inside his Mercedes. He wasn't sure how, but she managed to look graceful even wearing oversize cotton, abused denim and a pair of muddy boots. He took a moment to thank providence for the rubber floor mats he'd installed just the week before.

"It's just that I work a lot of hours," she was saying.

"Same here."

"It's hard to get out."

"At times." Mira, of course, had enjoyed spending time with him at Holland. He frowned.

"Not everyone understands the kind of commitment a vineyard requires."

"No. Not everyone does," he agreed. "Of course, there's a fine line between commitment and obsession." He moved to close the door, but she put a hand out to stop him.

"Which are you, Zack? Committed or obsessed?"

"I'm…driven," he replied, deciding there was a difference. This time she let him close the door, but the conversation wasn't over.

When he settled in behind the wheel, she said, "So, you straddle the line between the two."

Straddle? "I…no."

"Come on. Isn't that what driven is? Half obsession, half commitment?"

He wasn't sure how she'd managed to put him on the defensive, but he felt the need to explain himself. "I want to make a superior product. I want to prove—" He broke off abruptly. He wanted to prove to his father, to Phillip, come to that, to Mira, that his ideas had merit, that *he* had worth.

"What do you want to prove?"

"Nothing."

"You know what I want? I want another Judgment in Paris this time with Michigan wines, specifically Medallion wines, taking top honors," she said, referring to the 1976 blind tasting of California wines by French judges in which they won in every category against French wines.

"You aim high."

"Anything wrong with that?" she asked.

"Not a thing."

Zack started the engine. They arrived at her home barely a minute later. Thanks to moonlight and clever landscape lighting, he was able to admire the architecture inspired by Frank Lloyd Wright, with its wealth of rectangular windows and geometric motifs.

"I've got to tell you, this is a great house." Zack switched off the ignition and pocketed the keys.

"Dad liked it."

"But not you?" he asked.

"It's…big."

Something about the way she said it made him think the word was synonymous for lonely.

"It has seven bedrooms," she was saying. "My housekeeper is livid. My house only had three."

"I'm not following you."

"I owned a house on the water, a three-bedroom bungalow with an incredible view of the bay. I sold it and moved in here after…after I inherited the place. I don't really need all of this space." She blew out a breath. "But it's mine now."

"I like the way it takes advantage of its setting." The lower level and a three-car garage protruded from the side of a gently sloped hill. Rocky, terraced flowerbeds lit with small hanging lanterns angled sharply up to a wide, L-shaped porch that was braced with intermittently spaced square columns. "I bet these gardens are something in the summer."

"My dad's doing. He had a real green thumb, whether it was with grapes or herbs or black-eyed Susans."

That made twice she'd mentioned Frank. This time, Zack heard the sorrow in her voice. He envied the closeness they'd obviously enjoyed, even if he didn't envy her grief. Before he could think of something suitable to say, though, she was opening her door and getting out of the car.

He followed her up the steps to the porch.

"This is a Craftsman, right?" He'd always been a fan of that style of architecture with its solid look and angular lines.

"Yes. My dad had it built the year we moved here from the Detroit area."

"It's a very masculine design," he said.

"I manage to like it, anyway," she remarked dryly.

"It suits you."

"Oh?"

"No offense," he said quickly. "It's just that you're not, well, you're not a…"

"A what?" she asked.

He cleared his throat. "A frilly sort. And neither is the house."

"You only say that because you haven't been inside yet."

"Pardon?"

"You'll see."

Jaye opened the front door, ushered him inside, and Zack understood exactly what she'd meant.

Beyond the foyer he could see into the formal dining room. Busy floral wallpaper and a cabbage-rose area rug obscured the dark plank flooring and high wood baseboards. Not that either design element had much of a chance to shine in a room that had been stuffed with so much furniture. In addition to a mahogany sideboard and matching server, a massive curved-leg table stood surrounded by a dozen ornately carved, high-back chairs.

"The decor is very…unexpected," he managed when he recovered the power of speech.

"Unexpected? I call it hideous."

He let out a discreet sigh of relief. "I was trying to be tactful."

"No need. I'm not the one responsible for cluttering up the house's clean lines with all of these spindly legged antiques. I detest the stuff." She sloughed off her coat and tossed it over the scrolled arm of the English mahogany hall chair for emphasis.

"So, the entire place is decorated this way?" Zack hung his on the brass coatrack that stood next to the chair.

"Every room except the kitchen. Margaret wasn't much of a cook."

"You know, with the right furniture, this house would be a real showplace." He offered it as a casual observation even as an idea formed and excitement bubbled beneath the surface of his calm facade.

"Yeah, well, my stuff is in storage at the moment. Once I sell off all of Margaret's flea-market finds and auction-house antiques, the place will be decorated in a style more suited to its contemporary look."

"So you plan to continue living here?" he inquired. "I thought perhaps you would sell it since you don't need all the room."

"I'd like to sell, but I can't really bring myself to do it. It's so close to Medallion. It wouldn't be right to have someone else living here and enjoying the view."

He made a little humming noise as he processed her response. It wasn't what he'd hoped to hear, but he was relieved it wasn't an outright no. He glanced toward the stairs. "And you said it has seven bedrooms?"

"Actually, eight. Margaret turned one into a showroom for her dolls. She collects the kind that have eyes that open and close. Thankfully, she took all 212 of them with her when she left. The things gave me the creeps." Jaye shuddered.

Zack was only half listening. It just kept getting better and better. Jaye's house was perfect, absolutely perfect, for his plans to add a sumptuous, spa-style bed and breakfast to the winery.

He'd tried to convince his family to do something similar with the century-old mansion that had belonged to his great-grandparents. The massive Italian Renaissance–style structure at the southern edge of the vineyard had sat empty for the better part of three decades. It was in need of major repairs and renovations to make it habitable. With a little more investment, though, Zack saw it as a profitable venture. When he pitched the idea of an inn to his father and cousin, though, they'd shot it down quickly.

"We're winemakers, Zack, not innkeepers," his father had said.

Phillip had stood at Ross Holland's side, the positioning apropos. The two men always seemed to be in synch, while Zack felt out of step.

"Why are you constantly trying to push Holland Farms in directions that distract from our product?" Phillip had asked.

Zack didn't see the addition of an inn as a distraction. He saw it as a complement, and a necessary one as competition grew fiercer for space on store shelves and in restaurant wine cellars.

One way or another, Medallion would have an inn, but he didn't want to cut into the vineyard's prime acreage to build one. He wouldn't have to if he could convince Jaye to sell. That realization had him frowning.

"Have you lost your appetite?" she asked.

Zack cleared his throat and reined in his thoughts. "Sorry. No. Just...thinking." He sent her the charming smile that had always distracted Mira. Jaye's eyes narrowed, so he changed the subject. "Which way to the kitchen?"

"Follow me."

As Jaye had said, the kitchen was generously proportioned and gorgeous, its decor leaning toward modern with granite surfaces and professional-grade, stainless steel appliances. It was big enough, functional enough to accommodate a chef's needs.

"Much better," he murmured.

"Not a fan of antiques?"

"They have their place, but not in a house like this. Anything Victorian clashes with its architectural style. But your stepmother acquired some pretty pricey pieces from what I could see. They should bring in a decent sum when you sell them."

She eyed him warily. "You know antiques?"

"What can I say?" Zack shrugged. "My mother is a fan of late-eighteenth-century French furnishings. I started going to auctions with her when I was in grade school."

Jaye grunted out an oath. "No wonder Margaret picked you to buy Medallion."

He cleared his throat then, wanting also to clear the

air. "About that, Jaye. She never told me that you wanted to buy the vineyard."

"You know now," she said quietly.

He nodded but remained silent. What could he say, after all, that would soothe her bruised feelings? Unless he was going to offer to sell Medallion back to her. He wasn't. As much as she loved it, he needed it.

After an awkward moment she said, "I'll get started on the pizza."

"Need a hand?"

"No, but if you want to be helpful you can open that bottle of wine."

"Sure. Happy to."

She told him where to find the corkscrew and glasses and set to work constructing their pizza, first rolling out the premade dough and then slathering it with store-bought sauce. As she chopped mushrooms, green pepper and pepperoni on the island, Zack settled onto a stool on the opposite side and sipped his wine.

"Very good." He held up his glass to inspect the ruby color.

"It's one of our best." She set aside the knife so she could reach for her glass. After taking a sip, she let the wine sit on her tongue for a moment before swallowing. "Mmm."

Zack watched her throat work. She had a slim neck, long. The word *graceful* came to mind again. Despite her rough edges and mannish attire something about her appealed to him. Attraction? No. Merely curiosity, he assured himself. He appreciated strong emotions, strong convictions. Jaye certainly had those in abundance. She was so outspoken and so passionate about the vineyard.

Just about the vineyard?

He realized he was staring. Jaye stared right back at him, eyebrows cocked in challenge.

"It finishes well," he said and took another sip.

"Yes. Unfortunately, not everything does." She set her glass aside and started chopping again.

"No."

When the toppings had been arranged on the pizza, she popped it into the preheated oven and arranged two place settings on the island.

"So, why Michigan?" she asked without preamble.

He blinked. "Sorry?"

"Why did you decide to move to Michigan? What made you decide to buy my vineyard?" She settled into her seat, picked up her glass and gave him her undivided attention.

The wine's aftertaste soured as he formulated his answer. "I liked what I saw here. The potential as well as the challenges."

He also liked the physical distance. The miles he'd put between himself and California had been part of the lure. Jaye rolled the stem of her glass between her fingers and studied the swirling wine.

"You mentioned celebrating freedom earlier. I wasn't going to ask, but…" She shrugged. "Even though it is none of my business, I am curious. Freedom from what?"

"The past," he supplied. "I guess you could say I needed a new start."

"You'll understand if I tell you that your new start is damned inconvenient for me."

It was more than inconvenient. She'd made that very plain. And so he said, "That wasn't my intention, Jaye, so I'm sorry for that."

She nodded, apparently accepting his apology. He thought the subject might be dropped. It wasn't. She tipped her head to one side, "Sorry enough to sell?"

"No."

"Well, I had to ask." Her green eyes grew bright until she blinked and then half of her mouth rose in a sardonic smile that did little to erase the heartache he'd seen. "I didn't think you were, but I figured I'd give it a shot. I think it's only fair to warn you that that won't be the last time I ask."

"I know. And I think it's only fair to warn you that my answer isn't likely to change."

She sipped her wine and regarded him over the rim of the glass. "I guess we'll see about that."

CHAPTER THREE

THE wine was nearly gone and only one slice of pizza remained. The clock on the stove read eleven-fifty. Zack set his napkin aside and stood.

"Well, I guess I should be on my way. It's almost midnight."

"Afraid I'll turn into a pumpkin?" Jaye rose to her feet, as well.

"Actually, I'm afraid I'll overstay my welcome."

The man was in no danger of doing that. Jaye had enjoyed his company, so much so that she was sorry to see the evening end. Even as she wanted to chalk her feelings up to loneliness, a small voice kept contradicting her. Zack was smart, funny, an interesting conversationalist and an attuned listener. He'd make a good friend. He'd make an even better...

"You'll be okay to drive?" she asked hastily.

"Fine." He cocked his head to one side. "You're not worried about me?"

"Well, you know how it is. Wouldn't want to get sued for providing you with the wine."

"Gee, that makes me feel special." But he laughed. Jaye couldn't help it; she did, too.

Zack's expression sobered. "You know, that looks good on you."

"What looks good on me?"

He walked to where she stood, stopping just in front of her. "A smile. I don't know that I've seen you do that before."

"I haven't had much to smile about lately." She said it lightly, going for glib.

Zack nodded. He was oddly serious when he replied, "Perhaps I can remedy that."

He leaned forward slightly. Was he going to kiss her? His pose, the heat simmering in his gaze, both suggested as much. Jaye wanted him to, she realized, and so it came as a vast disappointment when his lips merely brushed her cheek.

"Thanks for dinner and the good company."

"You're welcome," she replied.

"I'll return the favor sometime."

"Oh, there's no need. Really. It was just pizza," she said, struggling to remain nonchalant.

"Another time," he persisted. "It would be my pleasure."

She shrugged and walked him to the door, feeling ridiculously out of sorts. It was just a kiss on the cheek. It barely rated as platonic. Hell, if he'd added one to the opposite cheek, it would have qualified as a polite gesture of welcome in many parts of the world. Why did her body seem intent on making more of it?

The night had grown colder, but she followed him outside and stood coatless on the porch in her stocking-feet.

"See you on Monday," she said.

"I'll probably be in over the weekend." The wind caught his hair, tugging it this way and that. His smile turned wry. "I'm not much for sitting in a hotel room playing solitaire."

As she watched Zack drive away, it hit Jaye that even though the man still had family, he was every bit as alone as she was.

Zack lay in the center of the king-size bed, hands stacked behind his head, and stared at the textured ceiling. It was past two in the morning, but he was wide-awake. He was still running on California time, he told himself, even though his insomnia had less to do with the clock than it did with Jaye Monroe. The woman intrigued him.

God help him, but there had been a moment that evening when she'd more than intrigued him. He'd come close to kissing her—and not just on the cheek.

"Not a good idea, Holland," he muttered, rolling to his side so he could flip off the lamp. "Not a good idea in the least."

Even having made that determination, however, when he finally slipped off to sleep, he dreamed of her, indulging in the kiss he'd denied himself earlier.

"So, what's he like?" Corey Worth sat across from Jaye in a Sutton's Bay coffee shop, her grin turning sly when

she added, "Mom said she saw a Mercedes with
California plates at the gas station the other day.
According to her the driver was incredibly hot."

"Your mother needs to get out more."

"Oh, please," Corey scoffed. "The woman already
goes on more dates in a month than I do."

Corey's father had died during their freshman year of
high school. The girls had been acquaintances at the
time, but because Jaye understood how it felt to lose a
parent, even though her loss had not been the result of a
death, they'd become fast friends. They'd remained close
ever since, even sharing a dorm room during college.

"Then *you* need to get out more," Jaye said.

"Why don't I stop by the winery later today? You can
introduce me to Mr. California and then maybe I will
get out more."

Jaye's eyes narrowed. "You would date the man who
is making my life miserable?"

"Depends on how well he fills out his clothes," she
teased. Then Corey turned serious. "Is he really making
your life miserable?"

Jaye wanted to say yes. But she blew out a breath and
shook her head. "No. Not exactly. I'm not happy that he
owns Medallion and I'm just an employee now."

"That goes without saying. But?" Corey prompted.

Jaye added a little more creamer to her coffee and
stirred it. The man made her nervous in a way that had
nothing to do with wine and everything to do with being
a woman. She wasn't about to tell Corey that, though.
So she said, "Well, he's not the jerk I assumed he would

be. He hasn't spelled out the changes he plans to implement, but I'm no longer worried that he's going to drive the place into the ground or do anything stupid."

"High praise indeed coming from you," her friend said dryly. "So, let me ask you this—if you met him somewhere else, under other circumstances, would you be interested in him?"

"Maybe," she allowed. She thought back on the conversation they'd had over pizza in her kitchen. "He's got a dual degree in viticulture and viniculture from UCLA. He knows grapes. He knows wine. He understands and appreciates the complexities of the business end of things. We actually have a lot in common."

"Work." Corey's mouth puckered on the word.

"Sure. It makes conversation easy."

"There's more to life than work or wine, Jaye. Shall I give you a for-instance?"

"If I say no are you going to anyway?"

"Yes."

Jaye sighed and waved a hand in resignation before picking up her cup. "Then, please, by all means, Corey, enlighten me."

"What does his butt look like?" her friend asked just as Jaye took a sip of coffee.

She nearly choked on the steaming beverage, laughter sputtering out even as she grabbed for a napkin. "That's one heck of a for-instance," she finally managed.

"Well, are you going to answer the question?"

One word came to mind and slipped out from

between Jaye's curving lips before she could think
better of it. "Prime."

Corey chuckled. "So you do notice more than grapes."

"I notice plenty of things, but Zack Holland is my
boss—at least for the time being. We didn't meet under
other circumstances, so my interest in him is and will
remain limited to professional."

"Hmm. Too bad."

The waitress came by and refilled their cups. Jaye
added creamer and stirred her coffee again. "Besides, I
doubt I'd be his type."

"And what would that be?" Corey asked.

"Probably you."

"Really?" Her friend grinned. "Do tell."

"I figure he'd go for someone petite and pretty." Corey
was blond, slender and all of five-three. She also loved
clothes and wore them well, so Jaye added, "And someone
who looks like she just stepped out of a fashion magazine."

Corey teasingly batted her long eyelashes. "Well,
thanks. I try. But you're pretty, Jaye. You have great
bone structure. You just need to play it up more."

Jaye held up a hand. "I don't have time for fussing."

"A little mascara, eyeliner and a sweep of blush
hardly qualify as fussing. And your hair—"

"Is easy this way."

"It doesn't have to be one or the other, you know,"
Corey said in exasperation. "With a good cut it could
be easy *and* more flattering. God, Jaye, you've already
got a color that a lot of women would pay big bucks to

achieve, and yet all you ever do is tug every last strand back in that tired-looking braid."

Because she was feeling tempted, Jaye crossed her arms over her chest. "No."

"My treat," Corey coaxed. "We'll go to that new day spa in Traverse this weekend, get a manicure while we're at it."

Jaye resisted the urge to look at her callused hands and close-cropped nails. Instead she grumbled, "Next you'll be adding that mascara, eyeliner and sweep of blush you mentioned."

Corey grinned. "I was thinking facials first. But, sure, makeup, too. Why not?"

I'll show you how to apply cosmetics when you turn thirteen. Jaye's mother had made that promise, but then Heather Monroe hadn't been around to keep it. Jaye pushed the memory away. She had makeup, an entire drawerful of products, most of which she'd bought at Corey's urging. She just preferred to go without.

"…and then I'll take you shopping at the mall. Your wardrobe could use an overhaul," Corey was saying, her gaze dipped meaningfully to Jaye's oversize shirt.

"This was my dad's."

"I know, honey."

Because she was uneasy with the sympathy she saw in her friend's eyes, she added, "I use his things for work clothes."

"Work clothes that you also wear out in public to meet your best friend for coffee," Corey said pointedly. "I don't want to seem critical, but you've really let yourself go since your dad died." She softened the words by reaching out to lay a hand over Jaye's. "You've lost weight, too. I'm worried about you, honey."

"I'm okay. Besides, you know me. I'll never be accused of being a fashion plate." Jaye shrugged. "I guess I'm still a tomboy at heart."

"I'm not expecting you to start wearing organdy skirts and high heels to work, but you used to take more care with your appearance. When was the last time you bought yourself a killer outfit and went out for a night on the town?"

Jaye scrunched up her face. "It's been awhile."

"We need to change that."

Her friend's idea continued to tantalize. It had been ages since Jaye had done anything remotely self-indulgent. From the moment she and her father had decided to start the vineyard, work had sucked up most of her time and energy. Since his death and since learning of the sale of Medallion, she'd barely taken time to look in the mirror.

Until Zack Holland had come along.

She shook her head, dismissing the man, dismissing her friend's idea. "I've got to get back."

"Of course you do." Corey's tone was resigned. "At least think about the weekend. It would be a lot of fun."

"I'll think about it."

But Saturday came and went. When Monday dawned, the harvest began in earnest at Medallion, and Jaye barely had time to take personal calls let alone the opportunity to head off to a spa for an afternoon of pampering. She did take some of Corey's advice, though, and started spending an extra few minutes in the morning applying a little mascara and liner to her eyes. But she donned the same loose-fitting clothes, since for the foreseeable future she would be up to her elbows in grapes—literally.

Medallion's operation was small, and they did things the old-fashioned way. They picked the grapes by hand, carefully snipping bunches of fruit from the vines and placing them in baskets to be taken to the crusher. It was a time-consuming process, and every available employee helped out. So even with the new title and duties of manager, Jaye found herself in the vineyard, traipsing the rows of grapes. She wouldn't have had it any other way, of course. But she was a little surprised to see Zack amid the workers the second morning.

It was the first time she'd seen him in blue jeans and she couldn't help but recall Corey's question about his backside. When he turned to talk to one of the other workers, her gaze dipped and her mouth gaped open for a moment before she thought to snap it shut. The man definitely did extraordinary things for a pair of faded Levi's.

A moment later he was walking in her direction. He actually looked excited, as if he felt the same sense of anticipation she always did this time of year.

"Good morning, Jaye," he called.

"Morning."

"Great day, huh?"

It was in fact overcast and threatening to rain. Still, Jaye found herself nodding in agreement.

"I told the workers that once things settle down and most of the grapes are in, we'll have a party to celebrate. We always did that at Holland."

At his words Jaye felt her stomach drop. "It's…it's been a tradition here, too."

"Oh, terrific." He offered an engaging grin, oblivious to her turmoil. "Then maybe you wouldn't mind adding the planning to your list of things to do?"

"Sure. I can handle the arrangements." Without warning, her eyes misted.

"Jaye?"

She glanced away, feeling foolish. "Sorry, it's just that my dad always took care of the party personally. With him gone, I…I just forgot about it."

"Understandable." Zack lowered his voice and reached out to lay a reassuring hand on her arm.

Jaye wanted to shake it off. But, God help her, she had an even greater urge to step closer and have him wrap his arms around her. She didn't just feel lonely. At times she felt unbearably alone.

"Zack…"

She didn't move, but he did. As if he'd heard her unspoken need he settled his around her shoulders. "I can see to the details if you'd like."

She blinked, seeking to banish the unshed tears along with her vulnerability. "No. Thanks for offering. I appreciate it. But I'll see to it."

"It hasn't been that long, Jaye. Cut yourself some slack."

His sympathetic tone had new tears threatening. "Dad loved the harvest." She glanced past Zack to the rows of vines that stretched across the horizon. "You know, I almost expect to see him out here."

"If you'd rather work at your desk—"

"I can pull my weight."

"I wasn't suggesting otherwise," Zack said. The arm around her shoulders tightened, pulling her closer against his chest. She swore she could feel the steady thump-thump of his heart. "I'm not questioning your professional ability, Jaye. But you're entitled to grieve."

She gave a jerky nod. "I know that."

"No one will think less of you. It's not a weakness."

"I know that, too." Her throat had gone tight, but she managed to say, "Thanks."

"No problem."

Then, to her mortification, a tear slipped down her cheek.

"Aw, Jaye," Zack brushed it away with his fingertips. "You're such a strong person. But you don't always need to be so tough."

But she did. She did. She was alone now. Who was she going to lean on? Zack? Because she actually was at the moment, she forced herself to step away.

"God, just what I need, to start blubbering while wearing mascara." She tried to laugh. It came out a hiccupping sob.

"I thought something seemed different. You have incredible eyes." After making that assessment, he appeared embarrassed. Reaching into his back pocket, he produced a clean handkerchief, which he handed to her. "Here."

"Thanks. I owe you."

"No. You owe me nothing." He saluted her with his clippers. "See you later?" It came out a question, sounded almost like an invitation.

"Sure. Later."

And she did. Once again that evening Zack and Jaye were the last two people to call it a day. They dined together again, too. This time the pizza was delivered and they ate it off paper plates while sitting in the small break room down the hall from their offices. They'd forgone wine, but the conversation flowed as easily as it had in her kitchen, and this time it veered into personal territory.

"Are you from this area originally?" Zack asked.

"No. I was born downstate in a suburb just northwest of Detroit. We lived there until I was in middle school."

"And your mom?"

As a general rule, Jaye never talked about her mother. Only Corey knew the details. But she heard herself say, "She left us a month before I turned thirteen. In her note she said she needed to find herself. As far as I know, she's still looking."

He made a sympathetic noise. "Sorry. That had to be tough."

"Nah. Dad did an incredible job as both mother and father, even if his face did bleach white the first time I asked him about sex." Jaye laughed, recalling Frank's stricken expression. Then she wanted to cry.

"Sex is a dicey subject," Zack said softly.

Jaye glanced over, distracted from her grief by the gleam in his eyes. "Isn't it, though? Some people have a tough time talking about it."

"But not you?"

"I'm pretty forthright."

"So I noticed." His lips twitched.

"Why beat around the bush?" She shrugged, but couldn't help wondering if that wasn't exactly what they were doing at the moment.

After a long pause, Zack changed the subject. "So, do you have other family?"

"No. Well, an aunt and uncle downstate, and some cousins scattered about the Midwest. I don't have any contact with my mother's side of the family, though. And I don't consider any of Margaret's relatives to be kin, a feeling that I can assure you is mutual."

"I didn't realize you were so alone."

"I've got the vineyard." She felt her face heat after saying that and she decided to redirect the conversation. "What about you? Brothers? Sisters?"

He dabbed his mouth with a paper napkin. "An only child, but I was raised with my cousin. My parents became his guardians after his folks died in a car wreck."

"How horrible for him. You must be close," Jaye said.

"You'd think, but no. Not especially." Zack's mouth

twisted. She thought he might expand on that intriguing response, but he changed the subject. "You know, I never would have taken you for a former city girl."

"Because I have more important things on my mind than the latest trends in fashion, hair and makeup?" Her tone turned chilly to compensate for her self-consciousness.

"No." He frowned. "You just seem so at home here. I can't picture you fighting traffic jams on the interstate during a morning commute."

"I can't picture me doing that, either." Then she admitted, "But I missed the city at first."

"Really?"

"We moved here in the dead of winter and lived in an old farmhouse just up from where we later built. The place was drafty and a little creepy." She shook her head. "I thought my dad was crazy."

"So what happened to change your mind?"

"Spring. And then summer hit." She glanced down at her work boots. Mud was caked on the soles. Seeing it there had Jaye remembering the early days when she and her dad had traipsed through the fields and begun making their plans. It had been just the two of them then and they both had felt bruised and a little disillusioned in the wake of her mother's bombshell. Little by little, though, they had patched up their hearts and moved on with their lives. "By the time fall came along I was good and hooked. I didn't even care that winter would be coming next."

"I know the feeling."

Because he sounded like he did, she asked, "What about California? Don't you miss it?"

"Sometimes," he averred. "My mother called the other day. Hearing a friendly voice made me a little homesick."

"And your vineyard? Don't you miss it?"

His tone was curiously flat when he said, "It was never *my* vineyard. My dad and Phillip—my cousin— we owned it together, but the changes I wanted to make, they weren't interested in."

"And so you bought Medallion and plan to make those changes here."

"Yes."

"And what are those changes? As manager of Medallion, I'd like to know."

"I have a proposal," he began, but then he stopped and shook his head. "I want to work out all of the details before I go over it with you. You're pretty key to the implementation of some of the changes."

"Really? Well, now you've got me good and curious. Can you at least offer me a time frame on when you'll get back to me?" she asked.

"End of the week."

She nodded. "I suppose I can wait that long since apparently I have no other choice."

"Eager?"

"Very. Maybe you can give me a hint."

"It sounds like the anticipation is killing you." His gaze dipped to her mouth when he said it.

She moistened her lips. "Chalk it up to fear of the unknown."

"Fear? No need for that," Zack assured her. "I think everything will meet with your approval."

"I don't know. I have high standards."

One eyebrow rose. "Are you hard to satisfy?" he asked.

"At times." Their double entendres had the room growing uncomfortably warm. Then to her mortification Jaye blurted out, "Are you involved with anyone?"

She watched his lips curve and his eyes seemed to darken. "No. Not any longer."

Something in his tone had her remarking, "It sounds like it was serious."

"It was for a while. We'd already booked the reception hall." He shrugged, and she figured the subject was closed, but then Zack added, "She's engaged to my cousin now. A spring wedding is planned."

"Ouch. That had to sting."

He nodded. "It did."

"But you're over it?"

"Over her." It seemed to be a clarification of sorts, as if something from his breakup had stayed with him. Before Jaye could ponder it, however, he'd turned the question around. "What about you? How close have you gotten to the altar?"

"How close?" She snorted. "Actually, I prefer to stay as far away from it as I can manage."

"Ah." He nodded. "Sounds like someone broke your heart, too."

She thought of her mother. Jaye wasn't willing to give the woman that much credit. "No. No broken heart. I just don't figure myself the sort cut out for matrimony."

Both of Zack's eyebrows shot up in surprise. "I can't say I've ever met a woman who shared your view. Most are eager to find Mr. Right. They make it their mission."

"What can I say?" She shrugged. "I'm one of a kind."

"Yes, Jaye," he said slowly, "I'm coming to realize that."

CHAPTER FOUR

WHEN Jaye arrived for work just before dawn the following morning, Zack's car was parked in its usual
spot. The previous night, when she'd gone to close the
blinds in her bedroom, she'd noticed that the light
was still on in his office. The man certainly was
putting in long days. Even as she was passing sleep-
less nights.

She was muttering to herself as she stomped up the
stairs. What was he going for? Workaholic of the Year?
She ignored the little voice whispering that she was the
defending champion.

The employee break room was just down the hall
from their offices. That's where she found Zack. He
was standing at the coffeemaker, hands braced on either
side of the countertop, and looking a little desperate as
the carafe took its time filling with steaming brown
liquid.

He flicked a bleary-eyed glance in her direction but
said nothing. His face, however, spoke volumes. His jaw

was shaded with stubble, and dark smudges bruised the skin below his eyes. It was just her luck he still managed to look gorgeous.

"What time did you finally leave here yesterday?" she asked.

He shrugged and scrubbed a hand over his prickly chin. It hit her then: the tousled hair, the rumpled clothes and bristly jaw. "My God, Holland. You slept here, didn't you?"

The coffeemaker gurgled, momentarily snagging his attention. Even though the pot was only a quarter of the way filled, he snatched it from the warmer. "Good enough," he muttered.

After he'd emptied what had already brewed into a large mug emblazoned with the words You Had Me at Merlot, he sighed and held it under his nose, as if testing its bouquet. It wasn't until he'd taken a sip that he finally answered Jaye's question.

"Yeah, I slept here." He pointed toward the lumpy brown sofa that was against the break room wall. "By the way, that couch has to go. It's hell on the back."

"Not if you use it for sitting," she replied.

One side of Zack's mouth cricked up in a smile that even a nun would describe as sexy. "What can I say? Sometime around three I felt an overwhelming urge to be horizontal."

At his words a picture of him in said position sprang to mind, accompanied by a completely inappropriate sizzle of awareness that zipped along Jaye's spine with all the subtlety of a lightning strike. Afterward, a tingling sensation lingered, as tantalizing as the man's smile. She swallowed and opted to ignore both.

"Maybe you should consider getting a room at a bed and breakfast in Sutton's Bay until you find a house. You'd be closer to the vineyard that way," she told him, pleased to find she sounded matter-of-fact.

"I've thought of that." He sipped his coffee. "But, actually, I've found a house I'm interested in buying. It's perfect for my needs."

Needs. Her own began to simmer. Jaye cleared her throat and inquired, "Is it nearby?"

"Very." He sipped his coffee again and seemed to study her. "But it's not on the market."

"Oh. Too bad." She tugged her braid around to the front and fiddled with the end of it, stroking it over the palm of one hand like a paintbrush. It was an old habit—a nervous one. Zack watched.

"Do you ever wear your hair loose?" he asked.

Jaye stopped fiddling. "Wh-why?"

He shrugged. "No reason. Just curious what it would look like."

"It would look long."

He didn't appear to be put off by her curt tone. "I'm sure," he murmured.

She felt the gooseflesh rise on her arms. "It's a pain in the butt to manage. Too thick. Too wavy. I'm thinking of having it cut."

"Don't."

The quickly issued command had her blinking. "Excuse me?"

"I mean, it would be a shame. It must have taken forever to grow it to that length."

"I've only had it trimmed twice in the past half decade."

"Hmm."

That damnable awareness was snapping again. Only, this time he appeared to be experiencing it, too. She tossed the braid back over her shoulder. "You know, it wouldn't hurt to make an offer."

"M-make an offer?" he sputtered.

"On the house," she clarified, trying to work up indignation over the way he was regarding her, when the only thing she was feeling at the moment was overheated.

The corners of Zack's mouth twitched. "Oh, right. The house."

"Why don't you contact the owners and tell them you're interested?"

"I'm thinking about it. So, you think that would work?"

She shrugged. "I don't know. But at this point what have you got to lose? A lot of people have a price at which they're willing to sell."

"That's exactly what I'm afraid of." Zack's rich laughter rumbled out.

"So, you think the asking price will be steep?"

"Think?" He shook his head. "I'm sure of it."

"It must be on the water." Even modest homes went for outrageous sums if they had frontage on the bay.

But he was shaking his head again. "No. It's got one hell of a view, though. One plenty of people would pay good money to enjoy."

She was truly curious now, her mind busily flipping through every nearby inland property she could think of. Nothing seemed worthy of such interest, though. "It must be some place."

Zack nodded. "As I said, it's perfect—"

"For your needs."

"Exactly."

"So, what are your needs, Zack?" Jaye wasn't sure what had possessed her to pose such a potentially provocative query, but she wished she could withdraw it when his eyebrows shot up.

"Now there's a question that could get a beautiful woman into a lot of trouble," he said quietly.

She gave her shoulders a negligent shrug even as her heart tapped out an extra beat. "Well then, it's a good thing I'm not beautiful."

"No. You're not."

Jaye's heart knocked unsteadily again, but for an entirely different reason. "Please, Zack," she said dryly. "Stop with the flattery. You'll give me a big head."

"You're not beautiful," he repeated. As if she needed to hear *that* a second time. But then he added, "You're striking, Jaye. You have a face that stays with a man."

He was studying her in a way that left her feeling self-conscious and exposed. The air in the room seemed to thin, making it hard for Jaye to breathe. She wanted to find an insult in his words, but, as compliments went, this was rated among the best she'd ever received. She couldn't stop herself from wondering: Had Zack found himself recalling her face?

"Striking, hmm?"

He nodded. "Striking."

As the silence stretched, she forced out a laugh. "Well, I guess that's better than being described as having a great personality."

"Jury's still out on that." But he winked and the mood thankfully lightened.

She decided to rephrase her original question. "Getting back to your house hunt, what exactly are you looking for?"

"Well, proximity to the vineyard is key of course," he began.

"I figured that much. And?"

"Well, it has to be large and well maintained. Architecturally, it has to have personality, inside and out. I want large rooms and plenty of sleeping quarters."

"Are you planning to have a lot of visitors, then?" She pictured a bunch of his equally stylish California friends coming by the tasting room and tromping about the vineyard. Maybe a gorgeous woman or two. He said he wasn't involved with anyone. That didn't mean the man lived like a monk. Because her upper lip wanted to curl, she nibbled on it.

"In a manner of speaking." The reply seemed oddly vague. But then he was saying, "This is a gorgeous area. I figure I'll get a lot of visitors."

Jaye snorted out a laugh. "Oh, that you will. Dad and I entertained our share of shirttail relatives and down-state friends over the years. Suddenly, people who couldn't make time for us when we lived a few miles away in West Bloomfield were eager to drive nearly four hours north to see us—usually at peak tourist times."

"Of course."

"I can't really blame them, though," she said. "The Traverse Bay area is a great place to get away. In the summer the main roads are crowded with tourists and seasonal residents. Pretty much every weekend in the fall is the same. The color brings them in."

"I can see why. The scenery is outstanding, especially this time of year," he agreed.

Jaye crossed to the window. The sun had just barely crested the horizon, but even shrouded in dawn's fickle light the landscape awed. "Fall's always been my favorite season," she confided. "Dad loved it, too."

Zack joined her at the sill. "It's a pity it doesn't last longer."

"Oh, I don't know about that. I think its limited run is what makes it so appealing. Kind of like Medallion's reserve wines." She smiled.

Zack's expression was a study in seriousness. "You've got a great smile, Jaye. A great…mouth."

He reached out and stroked the pad of his thumb over her lower lip. Unlike the kiss on the cheek he'd given her the other night, this gesture was intimate, loverlike. Apparently he realized that because his face flushed scarlet before he coughed and stepped back. "I'm sorry, Jaye. I shouldn't have touched you like that."

"No." *No?* She couldn't seem to make up her mind.

"I didn't mean to make you uncomfortable."

Try turned on, she thought, but waved a hand in dismissal. "Please. It would take a great deal more than *that* to make me uncomfortable."

"It would?" The simple question seemed to contain a subtle challenge.

Jaye decided to issue one of her own. "Oh, yeah. Much, much more."

"Such as?"

"I'll leave it to your imagination."

"You might regret that," he informed her. "I have a very vivid imagination."

"Then I'm sure I don't need to go into detail."

Jaye felt oddly empowered when his gaze turned smoky. This wasn't like her, engaging in verbal foreplay with a man she should consider off-limits. But, God, it felt good. It felt…liberating. It made her feel alive. Still, a smart woman knew when to leave, so she brushed past him with the hint of a smile tugging at her lips. Over her shoulder she said, "By the way, that's my coffee cup."

He lifted it, read the inscription and chuckled. "I didn't realize."

"I'm sure you just grabbed whatever was available in your sleep-deprived state."

He stopped her by saying, "No. I mean, I didn't realize you had a sense of humor. You keep it pretty well under wraps. Makes a man wonder what other things he might discover about you if you ever let your hair down." He grinned. "That's just a figure of speech, although in this case I wouldn't mind if you took it literally. Maybe I could watch."

Because the offer was tempting, she rolled her eyes. "Be sure to wash the cup."

"You can have it back right now if you'd like. Coffee's still hot."

"I'll get my own, thanks," she replied.

"Don't say I didn't make the offer."

Exactly what offer was that? Jaye wondered.

Zack watched her leave the room. He waited until he heard her heavy work boots on the stairs before he let out an oath. What had gotten into him? He had a feeling the question might be easier to answer if he asked himself *who?*

In the past few weeks at Medallion, he'd already become accustomed to butting heads with Jaye. She was stubborn, opinionated and used to doing things her own way. She also was dedicated, bright, a hard worker and a vital and valuable employee, even if she did sometimes still act as if she was running the show. But his interest in her seemed to keep straying well beyond business.

"Not a good idea," he told himself, and not for the first time.

Besides, she was far too single-minded. He'd been involved with a woman like that before. Neither his pride nor his heart had survived the encounter intact. He didn't plan to get serious with another woman for a very long time. When he did, it would be someone who could separate what he did for a living from who he was as a man.

The vineyard is my life. Jaye had told him that the

first day. At least she was up-front about it. Zack's ex-fiancée had left him to figure it out on his own.

And that brought him to another reason he needed to tread carefully. He owned the vineyard Jaye loved, and he planned to approach her about buying the home in which she currently lived. The home that had been willed to her by the father she still mourned. Those were excellent reasons to keep his relationship with her strictly professional. Involvement with Jaye on any other level surely would complicate matters. He couldn't afford complications.

Zack fully intended for Medallion to have the inn his father and Phillip felt Holland Farms could do without. Jaye's house was perfect for the venture. In addition to proximity and curb appeal, it was small enough to be exclusive and had rooms that were large enough to convey a sense of luxury.

Most people have a price at which they are willing to sell, she'd told him. For the first time Zack began to worry that Jaye's price might not be one he could afford to pay.

One hour and half a pot of coffee later, Zack was feeling more like his old self. The incident with Jaye in the break room basically came down to harmless flirting, he rationalized. He shouldn't have touched her in such a familiar manner and he sure as hell wouldn't allow himself to do it again, but it's not like they'd had sex or anything.

Oh, sure, he was attracted to the woman, but he could handle that. Besides, more than likely his interest in her would wane as time went by. Right now he found her captivating, enchanting, but that was only because she was a bit of an enigma. A woman who didn't want to marry? A woman who was sexy even when she wasn't trying to be? A woman who had him wondering what she would look like with all that glorious hair loose and her clothes tight? Of course he was drawn to her. What man wouldn't be?

He was standing shirtless in front of a small mirror he'd positioned on the windowsill as he shaved with an electric razor. He'd started keeping a change of clothes and other essentials in his office when his days had begun to stretch late. He'd figured at some point that torture rack called a couch would call his name, and it had last night.

He switched off the razor and passed a hand over his jaw, which was respectably smooth now. Just as he was reaching for his shirt a knock sounded briefly before Jaye opened the door. This wasn't the first time she had barged in without waiting for him to call, "Come in," but in the past he'd been sitting at his desk, fully clothed. He took his time tugging on the fresh shirt. It was small of him, but he enjoyed watching a flush creep up her cheeks.

"Hello, Jaye."

She didn't avert her eyes, even though she did mutter what sounded like, "Sorry."

"You know, I close my door for a reason," he told her.

"And I opened it for a reason." Jaye shrugged and then stuffed her hands into the back pockets of her ill-fitting jeans. The move pulled the baggy denim taut over a pair of slender but shapely hips and had him wondering about the contours of her thighs.

Zack dragged his gaze up to her face and forced his mind back to business as he buttoned his shirt. "So, what did you need to see me about?"

"I've got some bad news on the pinot noir grapes. We've got a mildew problem and it's not pretty."

He issued a mild oath. "How bad?"

"Bad enough. We're going to lose a significant percentage of the crop, I'm afraid. I've checked around at other local wineries. It appears to be a problem everywhere at county and peninsula vineyards this year."

It wasn't what he wanted to hear. A couple of recent vintages of Medallion's pinot noir had garnered promising reviews. There had been high hopes for this one. This time when he swore, his curse was not only more creative, but more explicit, and so he apologized. "Excuse the language, Jaye. My mother would be appalled if she heard me say that."

"I'm not your mother."

"Thank God." He hadn't meant to say that out loud, but it was the truth, given the thoughts he'd begun to entertain.

Jaye eyed him curiously for a moment before continuing. "Besides, that was my initial reaction, too."

"Any other varieties affected?" he asked.

"The cabernet franc and merlot look to be in good shape."

He nodded. "What about the pinot grigio and gamay noir?"

"They're fine." She came fully into the room, her gaze on the front of his shirt. "That's buttoned wrong, by the way."

Zack glanced down. Sure enough, he was one hole off starting from the third on down to the tail.

"So it is."

Jaye should have left then. She'd delivered the message she'd come to deliver. She had no reason to linger, but she remained rooted in place, fascinated as Zack began to unfasten the misbuttoned shirt, revealing a tantalizing bit more of that nicely muscled chest she'd seen a moment ago. He glanced up halfway through the job, and their gazes met, locked. His fingers stilled. Her pulse revved.

"Am I making you uncomfortable yet?" he asked, one eyebrow arching as he alluded to their earlier conversation in the break room.

"No." And because the one syllable came out sounding normal, Jaye added, "Are you trying?"

His jaw clenched for a moment and he shook his head. "I shouldn't be. Forget I said that."

"Sure. Consider it forgotten." Right. Like that was going to happen. Everything about the man seemed seared into her consciousness. Jaye was beginning to feel like a voyeur as she watched him continue with his task. But instead of excusing herself, she asked, "Need any help?"

His hands stilled at the offer, but he shook his head. "I think I can button a shirt on my own."

"I don't know. You didn't do so hot the first time," she noted.

He laughed tightly. "You have a point."

"Maybe I make *you* uncomfortable."

When he glanced up, his gaze was so potent it had Jaye's smugness vanishing.

"Maybe you do." He took a couple steps closer. "Are you sure this discomfort thing is one-sided?"

Jaye moistened her lips. "It would appear so."

He advanced again, close enough that she felt his breath warm her skin when he whispered, "What about now?"

"Nope. Still fine," she managed, even as his seductive taunt had fire shooting through her veins.

"And if I do this?" He lowered his head, stopping a mere inch from her lips. "Do I make you uncomfortable now?"

Something in his expression made her wonder if he was reconsidering, maybe even regretting his bold move. Or maybe he was giving her the opportunity to back away. Jaye knew she should. Like it or not, Zack was her boss now. In a very real sense, he controlled her future as surely as he controlled Medallion's. Even so she leaned forward, taking the initiative and sealing her fate.

Just before their mouths met she murmured, "Not even if you do this."

Nothing about the kiss could be called one-sided. Both parties were fully engaged. It quickly changed from a tentative exploration to an all-out sensual expedition.

Need flared and eclipsed reason. It made a mockery of Zack's previous belief that the more he got to know Jaye the less he would desire her. By the time the kiss ended a full five minutes later, his hands were tucked into the back pockets of her blue jeans, palms warming against a surprisingly curvaceous bottom; her fingers were tangled in the hair that brushed his collar; and he was sure of only one thing: he wanted more.

Green eyes regarded him with a mix of wariness and satisfaction. He couldn't decide which was the bigger turn-on.

"I've got to tell you, Holland, you do that pretty well," she said in a matter-of-fact tone as they extricated themselves.

It wasn't quite the response he'd expected, but then this was Jaye, so he said, "Thanks. And likewise."

"But it's not a good idea."

He knew exactly what she meant. Yet he heard himself ask for clarification. "What's not a good idea, Jaye?"

"Us…kissing or…anything."

Her hesitant response could hardly be considered a declaration. What's more, her use of the word *anything* posed tantalizing possibilities that his reckless libido was eager to explore. But he managed to grunt out an agreement as he began buttoning his shirt again. "No, probably not."

"Let's just call that a one-time thing." She blew out a breath and fidgeted with the end of her braid. He felt his shaky resolve start to falter.

"Want to make it a two-time thing?"

"No." But she moistened her lips and he could see the pulse beating at the base of her throat.

So he did what he swore he wouldn't. He reached for the braid and used it to pull her to him. "Liar."

This time when the kiss ended, his shirt was on the floor and he'd begun to work the bulky cable knit sweater she was wearing up over her head.

"I need a little help here, Jaye," he whispered.

He caught a glimpse of white satin and lace and some incredibly toned abs before she yanked the sweater back into place.

She pinched her eyes shut, looking pained. "Zack, we…we can't do this. Not here."

He backed up a step and tried to catch his breath. "Sorry. I wasn't thinking. I forgot this used to be your father's office."

"No. That's got nothing to do with it. We work together. Technically you're my boss."

There was no "technically" about it, but he didn't correct her. Ultimately she was right, even if he didn't want her to be.

"Let's just forget this ever happened," she suggested. "Not that anything really happened. I mean, we kissed."

He felt the need to point out, "Twice."

"Right, but no harm no foul. It was probably just a reaction to…to stress."

Zack wasn't sure what made him contradict her. After all, she was giving him a face-saving out. But he said, "And here I was thinking it might be attraction."

"A-a-attraction."

Her stuttering gave him courage. After retrieving his shirt from the floor he asked, "What? You don't agree?"

"It's not a good idea," she said again.

"Yeah, well, we've established that, Jaye. I believe we're debating the cause rather than the effect."

"What does it matter?"

A wise man would have dropped the subject right there. Zack was feeling strangely reckless. "Well, if you kissed me because you're interested in me that would make me feel better than if you kissed me as a way to, say, blow off steam."

"So, this is about male pride." She crossed her arms and angled one long leg out to the side.

"Call it what you want." He shrugged. "Well?"

"I'm not going to answer that question."

"Ah, pleading the Fifth?"

"This has nothing to do with self-incrimination." She huffed out a breath. "God! You make me regret acting on the impulse."

He grinned. "So, it wasn't just a reaction to stress."

"Yes, it was. It's the harvest. I've been working long days. I was releasing tension." She shook a finger just below his nose before he had a chance to speak. "And I'm not talking about *that* kind of tension, either."

"Okay, Jaye." She looked satisfied until he added, "If you say so."

Her lip curled. God, she could be a contrary woman. What did it say about him, Zack wondered, that it only made him want to kiss her again?

He loosened his belt and unfastened his pants far enough so he could tuck the tails of his shirt inside. When she swallowed and looked away, he decided he'd scored a victory of sorts.

"It won't happen again," she told him. "It never should have happened in the first place."

He nodded slowly, all of his smugness vanishing. "I know."

Long after Jaye had gone, Zack was left to wonder why it bothered him so much that she was right.

CHAPTER FIVE

JAYE bypassed her office and jogged downstairs. For the first time in her adult life she shifted work to the back burner and let her personal life take precedence.

"Corey?" She was placing the call from her cell phone even as she walked to her car back at the house. "Got time for lunch today? Yeah, everything's fine," she lied. "I just need a little advice."

Did she ever.

They met at a restaurant in Sutton's Bay half an hour later. Jaye planned to ease into the conversation, maybe pose a couple of hypotheticals to her friend first. Instead, a moment after their salads arrived she was blurting out, "He kissed me."

Corey blinked. "Zack?"

"Yes."

"He kissed you?"

Jaye scrubbed a hand over her eyes as the scene in his office replayed in her head. The mere memory of it had her pulse spiking. And so she said irritably, "Okay,

I suppose I kissed him. The first time. For heaven's sake, does it really matter who kissed whom?"

Corey's eyebrows rose. "There's no need to bite my head off."

Jaye fiddled with the cloth napkin that was spread over her lap. "Sorry. I'm just feeling a little…what's the word?" she murmured half to herself.

"Tense?" Corey supplied.

"Yes." Then Jaye's spine stiffened. "No! I am not *tense*. Definitely not tense."

"Oka-a-a-y," Corey said slowly. "Maybe I need to look that word up in my dictionary."

"Well, I am tense as in 'stressed out,' which is perfectly understandable given the time of year it is at work and everything else that has happened in my life during recent months." She leaned over the table and lowered her voice to add, "But I am not *tense,* if you know what I mean."

"Jaye, honey, I haven't got a clue. You're not making much sense."

"That's because *this* doesn't make any sense."

"This?" Corey's eyebrows beetled.

"Zack and me." Jaye exhaled sharply. "Haven't you heard anything I've been saying?"

"Yes, but apparently I missed something. Let me see if I've got this straight. Whatever is going on between you and Zack—and you do realize I'm going to require extensive details on that matter—doesn't make sense to you."

"That's the gist of it." Jaye glanced out the window. "Not that there is or could be a Zack and me."

"Why not?"

"Are you nuts, Corey? Isn't that obvious?"

"Apparently not. All I know is that my best friend, who hasn't been in a serious relationship since a three-month fling with Bobby Shumaker in the ninth grade, now has the hots for a gorgeous, successful man who shares her passion for winemaking. What's the problem?"

Jaye plucked at the end of her braid. Summarized like that it sounded so…possible. But she said, "I'm not his type. He's…he's not my type."

Corey rolled her eyes. "Oh, God. Not all of that type crap again."

"Well, you know me, Corey. I'm not a good bet for the long-term."

"Has he asked you to marry him?"

"Of course not," Jaye replied.

"Then what's the problem?"

"He's my boss, Corey. He owns Medallion and I work for him."

"That poses a bit of a problem," Corey allowed. "Why don't you give me those details now? Tell me exactly what happened, where, when, why and for how long." She bobbed her eyebrows on the last.

Jaye kept it short and to the point. "We kissed. In his office. Today. I'm not sure why and it lasted for, oh, about ten minutes."

Ten glorious minutes that still had Jaye's contact lenses wanting to fog.

"You call those details? God. I've heard you all but rhapsodize over chardonnay grapes. Give it up, girlfriend. What was the man wearing? What were you wearing?" Her smile turned devilish. "Where were his hands?"

Jaye couldn't help it. She sighed. Then she spilled everything. Afterward she touched her lips and admitted, "To tell you the truth, Core, I'm surprised that kiss wasn't detected on the Richter scale."

"That incredible, huh?"

"I'm still feeling aftershocks." Was she ever. "So, what should I do?"

"Well, you could keep your hands and lips to yourself, and pretend it never happened."

Jaye had already counseled herself on that approach. It was safe and it made the most sense. Still, she asked, "What would be option two?"

Corey's grin broadened. "What would it hurt to let nature take its course? You're both consenting adults. You're both unattached. He is unattached?"

"Yes."

"Well then, as long as all of the rules are spelled out clearly ahead of time, maybe the fact that you two work together won't be a problem. In the meantime, if you're not in any hurry to return to work, what do you say we run into Traverse for some shopping? Macy's is having a sale."

Jaye agreed, not so much because she was in the mood to try on clothes, but because she was in no rush to face Zack again.

Maybe the fact that you two work together won't be a problem.

She contemplated Corey's words as they traipsed from

one store to the next for the better part of the afternoon. Something told Jaye it wouldn't be as simple as that.

And it wasn't.

"You're not avoiding me, are you?" Zack stood in the doorway to Jaye's office, hands tucked into his pockets, a smile curving his lips.

It had been three days since their kiss, and she had indeed made every attempt to be in whatever location Zack was not. If he was out in the vineyard, she was at her desk. The moment she heard him coming up the stairs, she pulled on her jacket and headed out. She wasn't a coward, but Corey's plan to let nature take its course was too damned appealing, as unworkable as it ultimately would prove. Still, Jaye shook her head in response to his question.

"Avoiding you? What reason would I have to avoid you?"

He frowned. "None I hope. But I haven't seen much of you since…well, since the other day."

"It's harvest. You know how it is."

"Yeah. I know how it is." He stepped over the threshold. "I need to talk to you, Jaye. It's important."

"Oh, sure." But she stood and was already reaching for the coat that was on the back of her chair. "Can it wait, though? I have someplace I need to be in, oh, about fifteen minutes," she said, pretending to glance at her wristwatch.

He watched her intently for a moment. "It can wait for a bit. How about this afternoon? Got time then?"

"Sorry. We're short in the tasting room. One of the workers has a dental appointment. I agreed to cover for her."

"Fine," he replied. But her relief was short-lived. "I'll know where to find you."

What an awkward mess this was, Zack thought as he headed for the tasting room later that afternoon. What had he been thinking, kissing Jaye that way the other day? He wasn't one to act on impulse. Hell, he hadn't even made that kind of move on Mira until their second date. Yet he'd all but seduced Jaye in his office.

And she'd returned the favor.

Still it was unacceptable, he reminded himself. Unacceptable, inappropriate, untenable. He heaped on the adjectives in an attempt to convince his libido to cease and desist. It just kept pressing ahead.

Jaye was his employee and the one person who stood between him and his vision for Medallion. It was time to spell out his intentions—for the vineyard.

She was behind the large, circular bar when he entered the tasting room. He nearly tripped when he saw her. She looked…well, she looked different. Rather than her usual uniform of baggy jeans and a bulky unisex sweater, she wore a pair of fitted brown pants and a long-sleeved white blouse that tapered in at the waist.

Zack had suspected that Jaye had a nice figure. Hadn't his hands discovered some of those very curves? Still, he hadn't expected her to look quite so sexy. Of course, with most of the woman's height taken up in legs, how could she not?

Her hair was in its usual tidy braid, but even that had him wanting to groan. He'd entertained some incredibly erotic fantasies about unraveling it and running his fingers through all of that rich, cinnamon-colored hair. She'd applied more makeup, although nothing obvious, just a nice blush to soften the sharp angles of her cheeks and a neutral shade of eye shadow that emphasized her long lids.

He liked the subtle changes he saw. He liked them a lot, in fact.

As he watched, she poured a sample of Medallion's 2005 pinot gris into glasses for a couple of young women.

"This is a medium-bodied white. One of my personal favorites," she was saying. "You might detect melon and floral notes."

The young women sniffed, sipped and then nodded thoughtfully. He'd bet the vineyard they didn't have a clue what Jaye was talking about when she said the wine expressed the region's *terroir.* They looked like a couple of college coeds out for a weekend of fun rather than being true wine aficionados.

"Awesome," one said as her friend drew a smiley face on the paper menu they had been provided.

"What selection would you like to try next?" Jaye asked, recorking the pinot gris and putting the bottle back in the refrigerated case. Her movements were fluid and economical. They had him remembering the way she'd wound her arms around him that day in his office.

"Do you make any wine coolers?" the brunette asked.

A muscle twitched on Jaye's jaw. "Wine coolers?"

"I like strawberry or lemon-lime," the blonde added.

Zack stepped forward, deciding to head off an eruption. What the women were asking was sacrilege, but then neither of them was pretending to be a sommelier.

"No wine coolers, but we have an excellent barrel-aged chardonnay," he said. "It's one of my favorites."

All three women turned in his direction. Only two were smiling. Jaye's expression was guarded, her emotions impossible to read as she introduced him.

"This is Zack Holland. He owns Medallion Winery."

"I'm Mindy. We just love your wine," the blonde said.

"Yes. You do incredible things with grapes," her friend enthused. The brunette's smile turned flirtatious as she traced the lip of her glass with the tip of one finger and then proceeded to caress its stem. As signals went, it wasn't terribly subtle.

"Thank you," Zack replied.

She held out her hand. "I'm Stevie."

"Stevie. That's an unusual name."

"My dad wanted a boy, but I'm all girl."

He'd seen pinups with fewer curves. Behind the bar, Zack saw Jaye roll her eyes.

"Well, it's nice to meet you both. As for Medallion, it only recently changed ownership, so I can't take any of the credit for the finished product." His gaze veered to Jaye before adding, "Yet."

"We're in town for the weekend, staying just outside Traverse City. Maybe you could recommend a good place around here for dinner," Mindy said.

"And for dancing." Stevie smiled provocatively. "I'll need to work off all of these extra calories…somehow."

He'd have to be dead to misinterpret the invitation the attractive young woman was issuing. He was very much alive. In truth, Zack wouldn't mind sharing an evening with someone other than the news anchors on CNN, but Stevie was way too young for his taste—and far too obvious. He enjoyed subtlety. He enjoyed a challenge.

His gaze cut to Jaye.

"Well?" Stevie asked.

"Do you have any ideas for these ladies?" he asked Jaye. "I'm afraid I don't know the area well enough to make any recommendations at this point."

She rattled off the names and locations of several restaurants and night clubs in Traverse City. Something told him she had no firsthand knowledge of any of them. He stayed while the young women sampled the chardonnay. When they finished, the bolder of the pair handed Zack a paper napkin with her hotel name and room number scribbled on the back.

"I'll be up late if you're interested in coming by for a drink."

Stevie's smile told him that providing libations was the last thing on her mind. He coughed to cover his embarrassment, and tucked the napkin into his pocket. When he turned, Jaye was staring at him, her disdain obvious.

"Problem?"

"No." But then she said. "She's a little young, don't you think?"

"Old enough to drink, or are you going to tell me you didn't check her ID before serving her?"

"I checked," she assured him. "She was legal."

"Good."

"Barely."

"As a point of clarification, Stevie is not my type. I've made it a rule never to date a woman who was born while I was still in high school."

"But you took her number."

"I didn't feel the need to be rude."

"And they say chivalry's dead," she replied dryly.

"Don't tell me you've never been hit on."

"I discourage that kind of behavior when I'm working."

"Not always," he reminded her, and enjoyed the way she flushed.

"You said you needed to speak to me. Speak."

"I'm not a damned dog, Jaye."

"No. You're my boss."

Something about the way she said it turned his title into an accusation. He nodded slowly. "Yes, I am. As your boss, I'd like to speak to you. Now."

"Fine."

She stalked up the stairs, back ramrod straight, shoulders stiff. He followed at a more leisurely pace, hoping some of her irritation might dissipate. This wasn't the mood he'd hoped to find her in when he made his pitch.

She was leaning on the edge of his desk when he joined her in his office.

"Have a seat," he said, indicating one of the chairs.

"I prefer to stand."

He closed the door behind him and walked to the other side of his desk. The proposal he'd worked up was in a folder on the blotter. He picked it up.

"As I mentioned earlier, I have plans to expand Medallion's offerings."

"Do you mean wine?"

He thought he saw a spark of excitement light her eyes.

"Not exactly." And because he was in no rush to show his hand, he asked, "Do you have a suggestion in that regard?"

"Dad and I wanted to produce ice wine. There are only four locations in the world suitable for making it. We're on the forty-fifth parallel so this is one."

He rubbed his chin. "I hadn't thought about that."

"A couple of the other vineyards are doing it. One's had considerable success. In fact, one of its vintages was served at the White House a few years back. The label enjoyed a bit of buzz from that."

"I bet. But it would require some planning and the dedication of a portion of our vineyard. If all of the factors don't line up just right…"

"It could be a bust."

He studied Jaye for a moment. "On the other hand, I do like a challenge."

"I do, too."

"So, you don't believe in playing it safe?" he asked.

"Depends. I don't believe in taking unnecessary chances that aren't likely to pay off."

"That's probably smart," he agreed.

"So what do you propose?"

"I'm not sure," he said slowly.

"You're not sure? You're the one who called this meeting," she reminded him.

"Oh. That." Of course, *that,* he chided himself and then mentally regrouped. "Back in California I had a couple of ideas for Holland that my father and cousin unfortunately were not receptive to."

"Go on."

He decided to start with the less controversial of the two. "First, I'm going to add a creamery here. Medallion will offer its own wheels of European-style cheese for sale to the public. We can provide samples in the tasting room along with the wines and sell it at delis and to local restaurants for use in their menus."

Jaye nodded thoughtfully. "It certainly would be a complementary product and a good way to expand our brand." She pointed to the folder on his desk. "Do you have a detailed proposal worked up in there?"

"This is a proposal," he said slowly as he picked it up. "But it's for something else entirely. An inn."

"An inn?"

"Actually, more of a bed-and-breakfast, something small and exclusive and very luxurious. It would turn Medallion into a destination rather than a brief stop on an area vineyard tour."

"Where are you proposing we build this inn?" She

nibbled her lower lip. He found himself wanting to do that, as well. He forced himself to concentrate on what she was saying. "I'd hate to see acreage pulled from the vineyard to do it."

"As would I, which is why I propose to purchase a nearby site with a house already on it. The house could be converted with minimal fuss, I believe."

"Ah, this would be the house that is perfect for the needs you once spoke of," she supplied.

"Exactly."

She nibbled her lip again. "It must be close by or otherwise it would lose its appeal. Proximity is key, as I believe you said before."

"Yes, it is." He took a deep breath and decided to just say it. "Jaye, I want to buy your father's house."

Jaye couldn't make her mouth work. Words formed in her head, but they never made it past her lips to become audible. Zack's idea made sense. Perfect sense. It was something Jaye would have thought of eventually, she was sure. Still, selling the house would sever her last tangible tie to Medallion. She would have nothing left. Zack would own it all.

"This is the proposal I've worked up." He handed her the folder. "I haven't seen the house's bedrooms yet, but from what you've told me and from what I saw of the lower level, I'm sure they will be perfect after some changes."

Jaye opened the folder and skimmed through the proposal. The sum caught her eye. It was generous.

Make an offer, she'd told him. And he had.

Get FREE BOOKS and FREE GIFTS when you play the...

LAS VEGAS GAME

*Just scratch off
the gold box with a coin.
Then check below to see
the gifts you get!*

YES! I have scratched off the gold box. Please send me my **2 FREE BOOKS** and **2 FREE GIFTS** for which I qualify. I understand that I am under no obligation to purchase any books as explained on the back of this card.

316 HDL ENT4   **116 HDL ENY4**

FIRST NAME   LAST NAME

ADDRESS

APT.#   CITY

STATE/PROV.   ZIP/POSTAL CODE

(H-R-01/08)

7	7	7	Worth TWO FREE BOOKS plus TWO BONUS Mystery Gifts!
			Worth TWO FREE BOOKS!
			TRY AGAIN!

www.eHarlequin.com

Offer limited to one per household and not valid to current subscribers of Harlequin Romance®. All orders subject to approval.

▼ DETACH AND MAIL CARD TODAY! ▼

The Harlequin Reader Service — Here's how it works:

BUSINESS REPLY MAIL

FIRST-CLASS MAIL   PERMIT NO. 717   BUFFALO, NY

POSTAGE WILL BE PAID BY ADDRESSEE

HARLEQUIN READER SERVICE
3010 WALDEN AVE
PO BOX 1867
BUFFALO NY 14240-9952

NO POSTAGE
NECESSARY
IF MAILED
IN THE
UNITED STATES

Between it, the proceeds from the sale of her beach-front home and the money Margaret's antiques would raise at auction, Jaye would be set financially even were she not also earning a decent salary as the vineyard's manager.

"Well?" he prompted.

"I hadn't considered selling the house," she replied truthfully.

He apparently took her response to be a bargaining strategy. "The terms are negotiable. This is really more of a starting point than a final offer."

Jaye closed the folder and glanced up. "But you want my house. That's the bottom line. You want to buy it and turn it into a bed and breakfast."

"Yes."

And she wanted the vineyard. An idea began to form. An exciting idea that had her wanting to grin. She managed to bank her excitement and keep her expression bland. "And the terms are negotiable?"

"That's right," he said slowly.

"Good." She nodded. "I'll get back to you with my counterproposal."

He didn't look happy to hear that. "I see. Do you have a time frame?"

Jaye felt the balance of power shift and took a moment to savor it. For several months now she'd felt she had no say in her future, no control over her life. Finally she did.

Her lips curved with a smile. "Eager, are we?"

"Curious," he corrected. "Well?"

"I'll try not to keep you in suspense any longer than necessary."

"I appreciate that."

"Give me the weekend," she said.

In the end, of course, Jaye intended for the man to give her much more than that.

CHAPTER SIX

JAYE had asked for the weekend to consider his offer on her home, so Zack was surprised when she called him late Sunday afternoon and invited him for drinks in Traverse City to discuss her counterproposal.

"Sure," he agreed. "Have you eaten dinner yet?"

"I had a late lunch with a girlfriend. We've been in Traverse for most of the day, shopping."

It was such a typical female thing to do, yet he had a hard time picturing Jaye laughing with a girlfriend as they popped in and out of boutiques. He said as much.

"Generally speaking, I'm not one to waste time in a mall, but my friend's been after me to treat myself to some new things. I guess you could say I decided to indulge both of us today."

For some reason her reply made him nervous. Maybe it was her use of the word *indulge*. There were several things he wanted to indulge in when it came to Jaye, things that were strictly off-limits but still managed to slip into his dreams at night and toy with his sanity during the day.

"Well, I've seen what you eat for those late lunches of yours, so let's have dinner along with our drinks."

He almost expected her to argue, but she didn't. "Okay. Got a place in mind?"

"How does Minerva's sound?" The restaurant was adjacent to his hotel. He'd eaten there several times since his arrival in town.

"I'll meet you there at six," she said.

"Six it is."

Zack shaved for a second time that day and felt foolish when he couldn't decide what to wear. Should he keep it casual? Jeans and a sweater. Go for a slightly more sophisticated look by adding a sports coat? Or nix the jeans altogether and dress as he would for any other important business meeting? After all, that's what this was. He wound up going for option two. Showing up in a suit might put off Jaye, who clearly didn't buy in to the whole dress-for-success theory.

Having reached that conclusion, he still changed sweaters three times and dithered between a couple of sports coats until he finally grabbed one off the hanger and headed out the door before he could change his mind again. He blamed his indecision on excitement. He was eager to hear Jaye's response to his offer. He ignored the small voice that kept insisting he was also eager to see Jaye.

When he arrived at Minerva's she was already seated on a high stool at the bar, but it took him a moment to recognize the sexy siren sipping wine as the same blunt-spoken woman who held the key to his expansion plans for Medallion.

She'd said on the telephone that she'd been shopping with a friend. She hadn't mentioned that in addition to buying a new outfit or two she'd had a makeover of sorts. Her hair was different—shorter, although only by a few inches. But in place of the trademark braid, she'd left it loose. It fell in long layers around her face before cascading down her back in a tumble of cinnamon-colored curls that invited a man's hands to touch them.

Of course, her hair wasn't the only thing Zack wanted to touch. The cashmere sweater rated high on his list, too, especially given the way Jaye's slender curves filled it out.

She'd paired the sweater with jeans. Unlike the ones she wore to work, these fit. Even though she was sitting, he could tell they hugged her body in all the right places. Her long legs were crossed, one foot swaying lazily in time to the bluesy Norah Jones tune that was playing. He took a moment to admire the sleek boots below the hem. Their daggerlike heels would put Jaye at eye level with him when she stood. Of course, he'd already come to realize that, employee or not, the woman was his equal in every way that counted.

She glanced over, and their gazes locked. When she smiled his heart knocked out an extra beat. She'd never lacked for confidence. At the moment, though, she looked more than self-assured. She looked…satisfied. She lifted her hand to wave and he caught a flash of red. Her nails, he realized. God help him, she had them done. He'd always had a thing for blood-red finger-nails. How was he supposed to concentrate on business now?

"Sorry I'm late. I hope you weren't waiting long," he managed in a normal voice when he reached her.

"You're not late. I arrived early and I've had a very respectable cabernet sauvignon to keep me company."

He took the glass from her hand and sipped from it, watching her over the rim as he did so. Something flickered in her eyes, as intoxicating as the wine he allowed to roll over his tongue before swallowing. "Medallion's 2003, I believe."

A smile curved her lips. She'd gotten far less stingy with those.

"You're very good at that. I'm impressed," she told him.

For some reason he found the need to say, "I'm very good at a lot of things, Jaye. And not all of them have to do with wine. I try to be well rounded."

"Do I detect a note of censure?"

He shrugged. "That wasn't my intent. Just stating fact. There's more to life than wine or work."

"Well, wine and work are one in the same for us, aren't they, Zack? And they are the reason you and I are here to have dinner."

She was right about that. "Well then, let's see about our table."

They were seated in the dining room and ordered an appetizer and drinks, but he found his mind on something other than business. "Your day of female bonding was quite a success. I almost didn't recognize you at first."

"Thank you. I think." She pursed her lips. "That was a compliment right, right?"

"Definitely." The word was spoken with a little more vehemence than he'd intended.

Jaye's eyes narrowed. "So, what you're saying is that how I look right now is a *vast* improvement compared to how I looked before."

Nearly too late he realized the boggy territory into which they were heading. "Do I have to answer that?" he asked.

"A smart man wouldn't."

"Well then, consider me a genius."

Even so, in the room's low light he studied her face—the high cheekbones, wide mouth and proud tilt to her chin. She still wore a minimum of makeup, but then she didn't need much to enhance what God had given her.

"You're staring," Jaye said.

"You're stunning." Zack hadn't meant to blurt it out like that, but then finesse, much like business, had gone the way of her braid. "Sorry."

She tilted her head to one side. "Does your apology mean you're taking back what you just said?"

He chuckled. "No. I said it and I meant it. I stand by my word."

Her smile was forthright rather than flirtatious. "And a good word it is. You know, I was flattered a while back when you said I was striking."

"I remember."

"Yes, but now stunning…" She made a little humming sound. "That's even better."

The waiter arrived with his wine, which Zack sipped gratefully. Business, he reminded himself once again. Business. But then he said, "I think it's the hair. I've never seen you wear it down. God, it's long."

"I'm beginning to wonder if you have some kind of fetish for long hair."

"Absolutely," he readily confessed. The obsession seemed odd, too, since Mira's blond curls didn't extend past her nape.

"Well, I did have mine cut today, but not by as much as the stylist would have liked. He wanted to bring it up even with my shoulders in some sort of layered bob." She indicated the length with her hands.

"The butcher. I'm glad you held firm." Zack saluted her with his wineglass.

She shrugged. "I've never been the type to let other people talk me into doing something I don't want to do."

"No, I didn't figure you were," he said.

He admired her for that, even as he found himself wondering if that particular personality trait was going to wind up dooming his plans. Anxious as he was to find out, however, they chatted about other things throughout dinner. Not surprisingly, when the meal ended it was Jaye who brought up the subject of business. The waiter had just cleared their plates when she reached for the portfolio that was balanced against the leg of her chair. She minced no words.

"I like the idea of an inn for Medallion. Love it, in fact. And I think my house will be perfect with some remodeling and, of course, new furniture."

"Of course."

"I've brought the building blueprint and some photographs of the bedrooms." She passed them to him across the table. "I've contacted an auction house in Traverse City. Once everything has been inventoried and appraised, they will send out a moving van."

"You've been busy."

"I've been motivated," she corrected with a smile that he didn't quite trust. "Until the antiques have been carted away, you'll have to use your imagination to picture what the rooms will look like with more suitable furnishings."

He grinned. "No problem there. I have a very good imagination."

"Yes, I believe you mentioned that before."

One side of her mouth lifted, but she appeared determined to stay focused on business. He should be, as well. So he said, "Of course, I'd like a tour of the place, too. It won't affect my offer, but I am curious."

"That can be arranged."

"When?" he asked.

"Whenever is convenient for you. I'm hoping to have the antiques out by the end of the week or the following week at the latest."

"They should bring you a good sum," he commented.

"Believe me, that's the only reason I haven't hauled them out into the front yard, doused them in gasoline and lit a match."

Zack chuckled. "They would make one hell of a bonfire."

"It would burn for days."

"You could probably see it from space," he said.

"Hmm, now I'm almost sorry I've made other plans." Both sides of her mouth curved this time. Then she cleared her throat. "Getting back to the house, every bedroom offers an incredible view. The master looks out over the vineyard and enjoys its own balcony."

"That's a nice touch. Romantic, too."

"I guess it could be." She nibbled her lower lip thoughtfully. It was a habit of hers that had a disturbing effect on his body. "You could advertise it as a honeymoon suite and throw in a complimentary bottle of our best sparkling wine," she added.

"What about bathrooms?" he managed. "Do all of the bedrooms have one of their own?"

"No. The two smallest bedrooms share one."

"Hmm. That poses a bit of a problem." He pushed the candle that was in the center of the table to one side so he could spread out the blueprint. "Paying guests of the caliber I'm hoping to attract aren't going to want to share facilities with strangers no matter how great the view from their window."

"Both rooms have large walk-in closets." She tapped a finger to the paper to indicate the area to which she was referring. "Perhaps adding a second bathroom would be feasible using the existing space and pipes."

"Perhaps. I'll see what a contractor has to say." He rolled up the plans and glanced up. "So, I take it this means you're willing to sell."

"Yes."

"Terrific." He smiled even though what he really wanted to do was pump his fists in the air. One major hurdle had been cleared. Of course, a second one loomed. "I assume since you mentioned a counterproposal that the terms I laid out don't meet your approval."

"Your offer is generous," she began.

"But you want more money."

"Not exactly." Her smile bloomed right along with his apprehension.

"Then what exactly do you want?" he asked.

She leaned forward over the table. The reflected glow from the candle flickered in her jade eyes. "Part ownership of Medallion."

"Wh-what?"

Zack's stunned and not particularly encouraging reaction was no less than Jaye had anticipated. She swallowed hard and forged ahead. "I will give you the deed to my house in return for a share of the vineyard."

Across from her, he straightened in his seat. "I'm not looking for a partner."

"Neither was I."

"Jaye, I know how much the vineyard means to you," he began.

She cut him off. "Then you know I'm dead serious when I say my house isn't for sale under any other terms. I'm not looking for a fifty-fifty split here, Zack. I know the value of the business and vineyard acreage versus the value of my house and its property. They are not equal. I'm not asking you to pretend they are.

You will remain the majority stakeholder in Medallion."

"Gee, that's considerate of you," he drawled.

She moistened her lips. "I can be a tremendous asset to the operation."

Her heart sang when he replied, "You already are."

"Thank you. That means a lot coming from you."

"Well, it's true." He looked slightly embarrassed. "If you were to leave, you would be very hard to replace."

"But you could. You would. I want to be irreplaceable," she said. The word seemed to mock her. She'd never felt that way in her personal life, she realized. Her mother had replaced her quite easily with a new, vagabond lifestyle.

"So, if you can't buy it outright, you'll be happy with just a piece of it?" he asked.

She nodded.

"Look, Jaye—"

For a second time she stopped him from speaking. "It's a good proposal. A very reasonable one, I think you'll agree, once you've had time to truly consider it. So, don't give me your answer right now. Look over my offer and study the photographs and the blueprints. Feel free to stop by for that tour. The pictures honestly don't do the bedrooms justice." With that she stood and gathered up her belongings. "I'll see you at work tomorrow."

Then she left.

Zack watched her go, his gaze lowering and lingering. He'd been right about the jeans. They fit her every subtle curve to perfection. He blew out a frustrated breath and slumped back in his chair. He certainly hadn't seen Jaye's partnership proposal coming, any more than he'd been expecting to see the woman who'd made the offer look like something straight out of one of his fantasies.

That ticked him off but good. In fact, the more he thought about it the more irritated he became. How convenient that her decision to get all dolled up and leave her hair loose had coincided with their meeting. He didn't appreciate subterfuge. Nor had he expected it from Jaye of all people.

"I'll take the check," he called out to the waiter as the man passed.

"No need, sir. The lady has already paid it."

That bit of news capped it for Zack. She was playing him. He didn't like it. He wouldn't allow it. He was on his feet in an instant and stalking toward the restaurant's exit.

By the time he'd retrieved his keys from his room and his car from the hotel parking garage, he figured Jaye had a good fifteen-minute head start on him. Still, he managed to pull into her driveway just as she was stepping out of her car. He rather liked the image of her caught in his car's headlights. She could be the one off balance this time.

"Zack. This is a surprise." She offered a wary smile.

"Don't talk to me about surprises," he snarled.

"Excuse me?"

"You've got a hell of a lot of nerve, Jaye." He

slammed his car door shut for emphasis and stalked toward her.

"I'm afraid I'm not following you."

"That's because you don't believe in following anyone. You blaze your own path and expect everyone else on the damned planet to just fall in line behind you."

She crossed her arms, angled up her chin. "I'm my own person. I don't pretend to be something I'm not."

"Yeah, that's what I thought, too. And I respected you for it, Jaye, even if I found it damned annoying at times. Then tonight…tonight you sashayed into the restaurant looking like—" His gaze skimmed down. He swallowed. "Like something edible, and you tried to seduce your way into a partnership."

Her arms fell to her sides. "Seduce my way into a partnership! I can't believe you just said that."

"Want me to repeat it?" he asked.

"Go to hell."

"Only if you'll join me."

Her top lip curled, which, perversely, Zack found sexy. "Have you even looked at my offer?" she demanded. Then she shook her head. "You couldn't have. There wasn't time. Besides, if you had, you'd know it's fair. It's more than fair."

"But you don't play fair."

"What are you talking about?"

"You…this," he said, pointing to her. "You decided to hedge your bets. You know that I'm attracted to you so you played up that angle, leaving your hair down, wearing clothes that actually fit and flatter your figure."

"You think I did this for you?"

"Was there someone else you called and asked to meet for drinks?"

"For your information, I did this for me!" she shouted, grabbing a fistful of her hair.

"Right. Excuse me for questioning the timing of your makeover."

"The timing may seem suspicious, but it's true." Her voice lowered, softened. "I've been dead inside for months, Zack. I finally feel alive again."

Funny, the same thing could be said for him.

Jaye continued, "I finally feel like the future holds promise rather than just more of the same…" She motioned with one hand as her voice trailed off. No words were necessary. He knew what she meant.

He believed her, but he hardly felt pacified, since she'd essentially told him it was the damned vineyard that was responsible for her rebirth. He cursed himself as a fool for thinking, maybe even hoping, for just a moment that it might have something to do with him. But that wasn't what he wanted. No, he assured himself, that wasn't what he wanted at all.

"So now your future looks bright," he said.

"I think so. I hope so. If you'll be reasonable and use your head instead of your…"

"My what?" he challenged.

"Your inflated ego," she replied pointedly.

"Believe me, sweetheart, *nothing* on me is inflated at the moment. You have a way of seeing to that."

She huffed out an outraged breath. "Are you saying I'm emasculating?"

"You're…something." And arguing with her was more of a turn-on than he wanted it to be. He shoved his fingers through his hair and then settled both hands on his hips. "I don't think a partnership between us is going to work, Jaye."

"Why not? Because I'm not interested in sleeping with you? Now, there's a good criterion for conducting business."

Her tone was steady, but she reached up to tug at the braid that was no longer there. Zack watched her loop one thick curl around her index finger before she let it go and crossed her arms. She was nervous.

He decided to call her bluff. "No. It's not a good idea, Jaye, because you *are* interested in sleeping with me."

Strong emotions coursed through Jaye. Anger was the only one she was willing to identify. The man accused her of having a lot of nerve. Well, he had no shortage of it himself.

"Tell me you're not interested." He lifted his chin. "Go ahead."

"I'm not."

His rumbling laughter mocked her. "You'd make a lousy poker player, sweetheart. Even in the moonlight your eyes give you away. You're as turned on as I am right now."

"This is ridiculous. I'm not having this conversation," she snapped, intending to leave.

"Coward." The accusation was spoken so softly that it might have been mistaken for an endearment. It rooted her in place. "Come on, Jaye, admit it. You're curious, too. That kiss in my office—"

"Was a bad idea and I believe I said so at the time," she finished for him.

Zack wasn't deterred. In fact, he looked downright smug. "Well then, this is probably an even worse one."

Before she could fathom what he meant to do, he'd grabbed her by the shoulders and hauled her toward him. Her arms were still crossed and now they were effectively trapped between their bodies. She wanted them free so that she could shove him away, but a moment later they were and Jaye did no such thing. Quite the opposite, she wrapped them around Zack, reveling in his warmth and wanting so much more than could be had standing outside in her driveway.

When the kiss ended, Zack said the last thing she expected him to say. "I'll take that tour of your house now."

"Wh-what?"

"I need to know what I'm getting myself into."

He wasn't talking about the bed-and-breakfast. Jaye wasn't either when she murmured half to herself, "Me, too." Shoving the hair back from her face, she asked, "Does this mean you're accepting my partnership proposal?"

"Yes."

She should have been thrilled. This was what she was after. But something seemed off. "Why?"

"Does it matter? You're getting what you want, aren't you?" he asked.

She swallowed. "Yes. I'm getting what I want." And more than she bargained for. "What do you want?"

"Well, I want your house for starters. I don't want a damned business partner, but you've made it clear that's the only deal you're interested in making when it comes to this property. So, I've had to compromise." He shrugged negligently, but then his demeanor changed. "I also think we need to be clear on something else."

"And that is?"

"I want you, too."

She exhaled sharply. She wasn't as surprised by his words as the effect hearing them had on her body. Need rushed in even as her breath hissed out. "Jeez, Holland, and you call me blunt."

"It's a fact. One I don't seem to be able to change," he added, implying that he'd tried. "As your boss, of course, becoming intimate would be a bad idea."

"But as your partner?"

"Still not a good idea." He frowned. "But at least I will no longer be your superior."

"An objectionable word choice, but I get the point," she said.

"Good. Here's another point that needs to be made. I'm not any more interested in a long-term relationship at this time in my life than I am in a partnership."

She recalled the ex-fiancée he'd once mentioned. The ex-fiancée who was now engaged to his cousin. "She really hurt you," Jaye murmured.

Zack's expression hardened. "Mira wanted my birthright more than she wanted me, so yeah, that hurt."

When he'd relinquished his claim to Holland Farms, his wife-to-be had relinquished his ring…and found a replacement.

"Now she's marrying your cousin."

He gave a jerky nod. "She's going to be a part of what was most important to her."

"That doesn't seem fair," Jaye said.

His rough laughter rumbled. "Life isn't fair, Jaye. Surely you of all people know that. If life were fair, you wouldn't be asking to become my partner." He swept his arms wide. "You'd own it all."

"I'd own it all with my dad," she corrected. "If life were fair, he would still be here with me."

"You're right." His expression turned contrite. "Sorry. I know how much you miss him."

"He was a good man. He taught me so much," she said softly.

"Mira taught me some valuable lessons, too. First and foremost she taught me to pay close attention to people's motives. I plan to be sure I know exactly what a woman is after when we get involved."

"And with me you know, is that it?" Jaye asked.

He didn't say anything.

"That makes me sound cold," she said after a moment.

"Not cold. I appreciate your honesty. You want this vineyard."

That was true enough, but for some reason hearing

Zack say it made her seem so single-minded, so obsessed. "I have a lot invested here."

"As do I."

"It's more than money with me." She needed him to understand that.

"For me, too, Jaye. I have more than money invested here, too. I need to succeed."

"So you can prove to your family that you were right all along," she added for him. Left unsaid was that in doing so he would prove to Mira that she'd chosen the wrong cousin.

He nodded.

"So we're partners."

"In business."

"And outside of work? What will we be after hours?" she asked.

"When we start sleeping together, you mean?"

She made a little humming noise in lieu of a reply.

"Exclusive," he said succinctly.

"That goes without saying," she huffed.

"Sorry. I didn't mean to offend you, but I don't share. I want to be clear on that."

"I don't share, either, and I appreciate clarity."

"As I recall, you once mentioned that you don't see yourself marrying."

"No." But her heart felt suspiciously heavy as she made the admission. "I'm not in the market for a husband. Is that a problem?"

"Not in the least. I'm not in the market for matrimony at the moment, either. So there won't be any hurt feelings."

"When it ends, you mean," Jaye said.

He nodded and she felt a traitorous twinge of disappointment, which she ignored, forcing out a laugh. "God, Holland, we're a cynical pair."

"Yes, but cynical looks good on you." His smile heated her blood.

"You know, here you are talking about how things between us will end when nothing has even begun."

"Nothing?" The word came out on a silky whisper.

"Well, not much." She took a deep breath and added, "Not nearly enough."

Zack's grin spread slowly. "Don't worry, Jaye. I plan to remedy that."

Her body caught fire, but her voice remained calm. "Now?" she inquired.

"Shortly." He chuckled. "I believe in taking my time. These things shouldn't be rushed."

"No." She moistened her lips, tasted him there.

"We're winemakers. We understand the value of patience."

"It can make all the difference," she agreed. "Ready for that tour?"

"More than. Let's start on the main floor and work our way upstairs."

"That's where the bedrooms are."

Zack held out his hand. "I know."

CHAPTER SEVEN

THE harvest ended and the winemaking began in earnest. The grapes already had been crushed, with most of the reds heading to the fermentor where the primary conversion of sugar into alcohol would occur. The whites were pressed and yeast added to start the fermentation process.

After this was complete most of the wines would be moved to large, stainless steel tanks or upright oak tanks. The red wines and some of the fuller-bodied white ultimately would be aged in barrels. Jaye always found it fascinating how different kinds of oak could influence the taste and texture of the finished product, and so she eagerly embraced Zack's suggestion to age some of Medallion's chardonnay in barrels made from American and Hungarian oak.

"It will produce a rich, buttery flavor," he promised. "Trust me."

She did. Even beyond winemaking. Jaye was learning that Zack had no shortage of integrity. The day they began the paperwork for their partnership, he called a staff meeting to announce Jaye's elevated status as Medallion's co-owner, leaving out the fact that he remained the majority stakeholder. He also was careful to keep their more-intimate relationship under wraps at the vineyard, even though now and again she would glance up to find him watching her, his assessing gaze hardly fitting for the workplace.

Jaye supposed some of the winery's employees, especially those whose jobs brought them into close contact with Jaye and Zack on a regular basis, were curious about what was going on between the pair of them behind the scenes. Thankfully, she heard not so much as a whisper, though.

At the house all of Margaret's antiques had been removed and an auction date slated for later in the month. The place felt bigger, huge in fact, and Jaye felt her excitement building as she and Zack began working on plans for its transformation from private dwelling to luxurious inn.

Jaye continued to live there. Renovations would not begin in earnest until after Thanksgiving and wouldn't be complete until late spring, so Zack said it didn't make any sense for her to find a new place until then. In the meantime, he'd purchased a sofa sleeper for the break room and he passed his nights there. Well, part of his nights. The actual sleeping part.

In the morning, after Jaye arrived at the office, he made his way back over to the house to shower and dress in fresh clothes, which were stowed with his other personal belongings in one of the guest bedrooms.

"You could just move in," she bolstered her nerve to suggest one evening as he pulled on his coat and prepared to head back to the winery to sleep. They'd had dinner together and a steamy interlude while feeding each other dessert. Jaye knew she'd never think of apple pie à la mode in quite the same bland way again. "You do own the house now and your clothes are here. You practically live here, anyway."

He studied her for a long moment in a way that had her knees going weak. "I know."

"Then why don't you move in?" She lifted her chin, raising the ante in what was becoming a high-stakes game.

"That's a serious step," he said.

"And we're not serious."

"You know what I mean. Living together would change everything between us. I'm not sure either one of us is ready for that."

"We agreed to no strings," she reminded him.

"That's right. No strings." He nodded. "That doesn't mean we should be careless with each other. I won't be careless with you, Jaye."

She liked his answer. It touched her deeply. And because it made her heart knock and her eyes sting, she smiled and forced her tone to be light. "Don't worry. I'll be sure to return the favor."

On the afternoon of Medallion's end-of-the-harvest party, the telephone rang just as Jaye stepped from the shower. After wrapping her hair turban-style in a towel and securing a second one around her torso, she dashed into her bedroom to answer it. Corey was on the other end of the line.

"So, are you going to wear the dress?" her friend asked in lieu of a greeting.

Jaye eyed the bold red dress that was hanging on the back of the bedroom door. Even on a hanger it managed to look sleek and sexy.

"No."

"Have you even tried it on?" Corey asked, sounding exasperated.

"I have."

"And?"

Jaye couldn't fault her friend's taste. The dress was highly flattering with its crossover neckline, three-quarter-length sleeves and a hem that fell to the knee. Still, she said, "It's too short."

"It's not too short," Corey contradicted. "It's the perfect length. It's the perfect dress. When I saw it in the window of that boutique in Sutton's Bay, I knew it would fit your body as if it had been made for it."

The dress did, too, which was oddly part of the problem. "I appreciate you buying it with me in mind. That was really thoughtful of you, Corey. But I'm just not comfortable wearing a dress. You know that. I've never been comfortable in one. I'm a tomboy."

"No. You *were* a tomboy, Jaye," her friend shot back. "And that was perfectly understandable when you were a gangly teenage girl without a mother around to show you how to be feminine or how to enjoy your femininity."

"My mother has nothing to do with my preference for pants," Jaye stated, but even she heard the defensiveness in her tone.

"Jaye, honey, I've seen pictures of Heather. Just because you look like your mother doesn't mean you are her or will become her."

Jaye studied her reflection in the mirror above her bureau. Her mother's face stared back. "I know that."

"Then start acting like you know that. Wear the damned dress tonight. You're an attractive woman with a successful career and a gorgeous man in your life." Corey, of course, was privy to the shift in Jaye and Zack's relationship. "It's time to move past your youthful inhibitions."

"Are you done, Dr. Phil?" she asked dryly, hoping to divert the conversation with humor.

Corey didn't follow her lead, though. For a third time she pleaded, "Wear the dress, Jaye. You have killer legs. Show them off. Zack will thank you for it."

"He does like my legs," Jaye murmured.

"He likes more than that, honey."

Jaye's heart fluttered at hearing the simple statement. The reaction made her nervous. In truth, a lot of things about her relationship with Zack made her nervous.

"So, are you going to wear it?" Corey asked, after a moment.

"I'll give it some more thought," she hedged.

Apparently mollified, Corey switched the subject. "What are you going to do with your hair?"

"I figured I'd braid it," Jaye replied dryly. Before her friend could sputter out a reply, she added, "Come early, okay, Core? I want to introduce you to Zack without a million people milling around."

Jaye decided against wearing the dress. Corey's irritation, though, was apparently forgotten when she saw what Jaye had selected instead.

"Nice. Very nice," her friend enthused when Jaye opened the door.

"You're not mad about the dress?" she asked, just to be sure.

"No."

"I left the tags on it. You can return it."

"Keep it. I'm sure you'll find another occasion to wear it for Zack in the future."

"Corey—"

"Keep it, Jaye. At some point, I promise you, you're going to feel comfortable in that dress. In the meantime, this outfit is stunning."

"Stunning," Jaye murmured, recalling that Zack had once used that same adjective to describe her. "Thanks."

Jaye felt stunning. The wide-legged black silk trousers had the same loose flow of a long skirt. She'd paired them with a jade-colored jacket of the same fabric. The cut was flattering, crossing over in much the same way the dress had and then nipping in at the waist before flaring out slightly at the hip.

She'd left her hair down, which she was doing more often lately, although she still pulled it back for work. She'd also applied a bit more eye makeup than usual.

"Is it too much?" she asked Corey when her friend continued to stare at her.

"No."

"Are you sure?"

"Jaye, you look incredible."

"But it's not…too much. I don't want anyone to think I spent the day primping."

"Would that be such a bad thing?" Then Corey shook her head. "Forget I asked that. To answer your question, it's not too much. Your look remains understated, but now it's also elegant and sophisticated."

Jaye's mood brightened. She liked those adjectives as much as she liked stunning. "Thanks."

"It's also perfectly fitting given your new status," Corey added.

"No one knows Zack and I are seeing each other," Jaye reminded her.

"Actually, I was referring to your status as Medallion's co-owner."

"Oh. That."

A grin bloomed on her friend's pretty face. Laughter followed.

"What's so funny?" Jaye demanded.

"I think that's the first time I can remember you letting something, or in this case some*one,* come before the vineyard in your mind. I can't wait to meet the man who managed that."

Jaye rolled her eyes. Inside, however, Corey's teasing comment further stoked her nerves.

Zack had been generous with the budget for the party, which in addition to celebrating the end of the harvest was intended to officially introduce him to the community, and Jaye had spent every dime he'd allocated. She had not only hired one of the area's top caterers to see to food and refreshments, she'd hired live entertainment.

Corey, who got out much more often than Jaye did, had recommended the band. Jaye took one look at the lead guitar player's tight jeans and ripped abs and figured she knew why. But actually the band was very good and played a range of music from classic rock and rhythm-and-blues to pop and even some jazz. Its members were warming up when Jaye and Corey stepped into the tasting room, which had been decorated with tea lights and hanging paper lanterns to create a more festive atmosphere. Zack was on the far side of the room talking with a couple of Medallion workers. He glanced up when Jaye and Corey entered.

"Oh, my God!" Corey grabbed Jaye's arm. "That's got to be him."

It was, but she still asked, "Why do you say that?"

"If it's not, the way he's looking at you could get him arrested." Corey fanned herself and muttered half under her breath, "I think I hate you," as Zack approached.

He was wearing a charcoal suit that accentuated his broad shoulders and lean hips. The white shirt and silk tie said businessman, but the hair curling up at his collar shouted something far less structured and stuffy. Sexy was the word that kept coming to Jaye's mind.

"Good evening, ladies," he said when he reached them. To Jaye, he added a simple, "Very nice."

"Thanks." God help her, she was pretty sure she blushed. "Zack, I want to introduce you to my friend, Corey Worth. Corey and I have known one another since high school."

"It's nice to meet you," he said, shaking Corey's hand.

"Likewise," Corey replied. "Jaye has told me a lot about you."

"Yes, well, don't believe half of it. You know how Jaye is prone to exaggeration," he teased.

"Not in this case." Corey grinned. "In fact, I'd say she played down some pretty key details."

His gaze flicked to Jaye, who felt her face heat a second time.

Mustering a thin smile, she asked, "Drink, anyone?"

Interesting, Zack thought, as they headed for the bar. Jaye appeared to be blushing. Again.

"Maybe we could have a toast," Corey suggested. "To friends, old and new."

Half a dozen black-vested bartenders were positioned behind the circular bar that normally only offered wine. Tonight, in addition to all of Medallion's vintages, the bar was fully stocked with every sort of beverage.

"What would you like?" Zack asked.

"I'll have a gin and tonic, please," Corey said. "Throw in an extra lime," she told the man.

"Just water for me," Jaye said.

"Make that two waters," Zack told the bartender.

"Wow. You two certainly know how to walk on the wild side," Corey teased.

"That will come later," he replied with a wink. His tone was light, but he didn't mean the words as a joke.

"Night's young," Jaye agreed.

She pushed a handful of hair back from her face so she could take a sip of water. The gesture was practical and ridiculously sexy. Zack had been looking forward to this night for weeks, happy to reward Medallion's staff for their hard work and eager to officially meet his neighbors and competitors in Leelanau's wine community. But at that moment all he wanted to do was cancel the party, send Corey on her way and retreat to the house so he could find out what Jaye had on underneath those flowing pants and that cinched blouse.

Truth be told, he'd expected her to wear a dress. The occasion called for it. The fact that she hadn't was somehow better. He liked that she remained a little defiant of convention. He liked that nothing about her was ever predictable. Even her moods couldn't be anticipated. Sometimes she was so vulnerable; other times nothing could shake her confidence.

"Why are you looking at me like that?" Jaye whispered.

Zack blinked. "How am I looking at you?"

"I don't know." Her laughter started bold before turning self-conscious. "Like you've never seen me before."

"I'm not always sure I know you," he whispered in

reply. The admission didn't trouble him as much as the fact that lately he'd found himself wanting to know Jaye's every last secret, dream and desire.

She gave him a funny look. "I'm not sure I know what you mean?"

Zack shook his head. "Nothing. Never mind." He smiled at Corey, who was pretending not to listen in on their baffling conversation. "So, you and Jaye have been friends since high school." His grin turned devilish. "Got any pictures from slumber parties?"

An hour later most of their guests had arrived and were milling about, enjoying drinks and helping themselves to the assortment of appetizers that had been set out on a long buffet table. For now the band had been asked to keep it mellow and the volume low enough to allow for conversation. Later in the evening they would kick it into high gear so couples could dance. During a lull between songs, Zack stepped to the stage area to officially welcome Medallion's guests.

"Good evening and thank you for coming tonight." He waited a moment until he was sure he had everyone's full attention. "As many of you know, I'm Zack Holland. I'm not new to winemaking. I grew up on a vineyard and worked my first harvest when I was still in grade school. But I am new to Michigan. I'm originally from California and I appreciate it that you've not held that against me." Muffled laughter greeted his quip.

"Tonight we're celebrating. We're celebrating a good

harvest thanks to the hard work of Medallion's crew. Frank Monroe knew what he was doing when he hired these people. They are smart, skilled and, above all else, dedicated. They've given me one hundred percent from the first day I came to Medallion. And so I want to thank them." He raised the glass of pinot noir he held and glanced around the room, taking care to make eye contact with as many of Medallion's people as possible.

He saved Jaye for last.

"We're also celebrating something else tonight. As all of you know, Medallion was a family-run business before, well, before Frank's untimely death. His daughter, Jaye, for reasons that don't really matter at this point, didn't inherit the vineyard at his passing. I don't think I'm talking out of turn to say that didn't sit well with a lot of folks around here, least of all Jaye. In fact, on my first day at Medallion she offered to buy me out.

"I told her no then and the other times she asked. I like what I see here. I like the Leelanau wine community and the friendly rivalry between vintners in the county and those on the Mission Peninsula. I have no plans to sell and go elsewhere. But Jaye, well, she can be pretty persistent."

As he'd anticipated, his understatement drew shouts of laughter. The woman under discussion, however, wasn't smiling, even when he winked at her.

Zack went on. "I came here with big plans for Medallion, things I've wanted to try in the past but was unable to implement. Jaye made me see the value of having a partner while attempting them. That's what she is now—co-owner of Medallion Winery."

Applause erupted along with chatter. Guests standing nearest to Jaye slapped her on the back or reached out to shake her hand and offer their congratulations. Zack waited until the room had quieted before continuing.

"So, in addition to raising your glasses to a good harvest, I ask you to raise them to Jaye. A man couldn't ask for a better partner. I count myself lucky to have her." The words were true…on more levels than he cared to consider at this point. He lifted his glass. "To Jaye."

While he'd made the announcement, her expression had changed from confusion to wariness and finally embarrassment. But she was touched, too, and rightly proud. He could see both in the way one corner of her mouth lifted and her chin angled up slightly. When he left the stage and joined her, stopping first to pick up a bouquet of red roses from behind the bar, her expression turned vulnerable.

The band had resumed playing and conversations returned to full swing when he reached her by the big window that offered a glimpse of Medallion's winemaking operation. Corey had seen him coming and discreetly excused herself.

"These are for you." He handed her the flowers.

"Roses." She buried her face in the blooms, her cheeks turning as richly hued as the petals. "I don't know that anyone has ever given me roses before. Thank you."

Because he wanted to lean over and kiss her, Zack cleared his throat. "You're welcome."

"Why did you do that?"

"Flowers seemed appropriate for the occasion," Zack said.

"No. I mean, why did you announce our partnership in such a public way."

"Does it bother you?"

She shook her head. "Hardly. But it wasn't necessary. Everyone at Medallion already knew."

"Yes, but the other Leelanau vintners didn't. I believe in playing fair," he added.

"Fair?" Jaye's brow puckered. "I'm afraid I don't understand what you mean."

"The competition has a right to know what they're up against." He grinned as he clinked the rim of his wineglass against hers.

"Thanks."

He sobered. "I meant what I said, Jaye. You make one hell of a partner."

"Same goes. I've never met anyone as passionate about the business as I am."

"I am passionate about wine," he agreed. "Among other things." His gaze dipped to her lips, lingering. "You know, it's getting warm in here."

"I noticed that."

"Yeah? Care to step outside for some fresh air?"

"Great minds," she murmured. "I was just about to ask you the same thing."

Jaye didn't bother with her coat even though the evening was chilly. Outside, a few guests milled about on the patio, indulging in a cigarette since smoking was prohibited indoors. When Jaye stopped at one of the tables, Zack took her hand.

"Come on."

"Where are we going?" she asked.

"Someplace a little more private," he whispered.

He tucked her hand into the crook of his arm. Moonlight lent a magical quality to the evening as he steered her down the brick walkway that led to the cellar where the wines were aged and stored.

"After you," he said, opening the door.

The cellar was built into the side of a hill. The building was utilitarian and not particularly pleasing to the eye, but it provided the privacy Zack wanted. No guest would see them here. Inside, the roof was made of variegated steel that curved in an arch and caused their voices to echo. Zack flipped on the lights and closed the door behind them, further ensuring that the wine-filled wooden barrels and moveable shelves of bottled vintages would be their only company.

Just to the left of the entrance, resting on the lid of a linen-covered barrel, stood an opened bottle of Medallion's semidry Riesling and two clean glasses.

Jaye's eyebrows cocked up when she spied the arrangement, and amusement shimmered in her green eyes when she turned to him. "A little presumptuous, aren't you, Holland?"

Zack shook his head. "If I were presumptuous I would have had the couch from the break room moved in here."

The suggestive comment earned her laughter.

He went on. "I prefer to think of myself as hopeful.

As in, I was hopeful that at some point this evening I would be able to steal you away for a few minutes."

"Ah. I see the difference."

"Do you mind?" he asked.

"Not in the least." She set the roses aside and picked up a glass and held it out for him to pour the wine.

He filled it and then his own. After taking a sip of the medium-bodied white he said, "You know, when we first met, I never would have guessed we would be so…compatible."

"I've changed a little." Her free hand slid over her hair in an absent gesture before tucking a hank of it behind her ear. "I think I've mellowed a bit."

"Mellowed?"

"A bit," she said again.

Zack couldn't help it. He laughed. "No you haven't, Jaye." Her eyes narrowed, so he pressed ahead. "Before you get your back up, that's a good thing. I don't want you mellow. Half of your appeal is your spunk."

"Spunk." Her lips twisted. "I think I liked it better when you referred to me as striking and stunning."

"See, there you go. You're opinionated and stubborn." When she frowned, he took her wine, set it aside with his and stepped forward. "Of course, your being so easy on the eye makes up for the fact that you're so damned hardheaded."

"Easy on the eye?" She was still frowning.

"Stunning," he corrected.

"Well, now, anyway. When we first met I was a bit rough around the edges."

Because she was being earnest he tucked away his grin. Vulnerable. That's what she was at the moment. "Then, now. You've always had my attention. Not that I don't especially like your appearance now. But something about you grabbed me from day one."

"I thought you were pretty hot, too." Her lips twitched.

"Yeah?"

"In a very California way," she amended.

"And what is that exactly, Ms. Midwest?"

"Oh, you know. Longer hair, relaxed style. And I thought you had a great butt." Her hands slid over the body part in question. "Still, I didn't expect us to end up involved, either in business or like this."

"Can't say I saw either coming myself," Zack agreed as he leaned in to kiss her. As their lips met, he added, "But I consider both to be a bonus."

By the time the kiss ended, Jaye swore she saw fireworks. The man certainly knew how to use his mouth.

"Do you think it would be bad form for the hosts not to return to the party?" she asked as the air sawed in and out of her lungs.

He rested his forehead against hers and struggled to catch his breath, as well. "Yes. Exceedingly."

"Damn. I thought so, too, but I figured I should get a second opinion. I guess this means we should return to the party." She stepped away, but he caught her hand and used it to tug her back into his embrace.

"We have obligations," he noted. His teeth nipped her jaw.

"Mmm." She sighed, because of those obligations and because of the effect his teeth were having on her heart rate. "People are probably already wondering where we are."

"I know." He stopped, but only so he could push her hair back for better access to her neck. His breath was hot on her skin. "What do you say we keep them in the dark for a few more minutes?"

"Only a few minutes?" she asked.

Zack chuckled and reached for the sash on her blouse. "Well, maybe a little longer."

It was a good hour before they returned to the party, slipping in from opposite doors.

CHAPTER EIGHT

As the weeks passed, their relationship changed, taking on greater depth and character, much like the wines that were aging in Medallion's cellar.

They had a lot in common—much more than Jaye could have imagined at the beginning. They liked the same film noir movies and were both fans of old *Seinfeld* reruns. When they had time they preferred reading medical thrillers to nonfiction, and when it came to dessert anything containing chocolate appealed to their palates.

Their views diverged on politics, but even in this they had something in common: they enjoyed debating the issues. The side bonus was that their passionate arguments often inspired heat of a more basic nature.

Jaye thought she finally understood why her father had opted to attempt matrimony again after her mother's heart-shattering abandonment. It was good not to be alone. It was good to have another adult to share meals with and evening conversation.

And then, of course, there was the sex…

Zack was a considerate and thorough lover, giving as much as he demanded in return, and Jaye matched his passion. Sometimes she took the lead, initiating their lovemaking. Other times she was content in the role of pupil, eager to discover what Zack would do next. The man was nothing if not inventive in bed, and it turned out she had quite a creative streak under the covers herself.

For the first time in her life, Jaye felt confident in her femininity. She enjoyed being a woman, so much so that she no longer thought of herself as a tomboy. She wasn't dressing the part, either, not even at work. Her father's oversize shirts had been relegated to a closet. She didn't need them to feel close to Frank. He was all around her—in the wines, the grapevines, the tasting room, the house.

Her dad would be pleased with the changes underway at Medallion, Jaye was sure. And he would be proud of the role she was playing in them. She knew he would like Zack, too, even if Frank wouldn't approve of the couple's intimate relationship, given the lack of a long-term commitment.

In truth, that was starting to bother Jaye, as well. Sometimes, in the wee hours of the morning, when Zack roused from slumber and slipped from her bed, she found herself wishing that he would stay. Indeed she found herself wishing for something far more permanent and enduring than their comfortable dinners and passionate evening encounters. She, the woman who had always assumed she wasn't cut out for marriage.

A couple of times during their lovemaking she'd nearly blurted out feelings that were much bigger and far scarier than anything she'd experienced before. On both occasions she'd managed to tamp down her wayward emotions before she embarrassed herself. She chalked up those weak moments to hormones and sex. After all, everyone knew that during the height of passion people often said or thought things they didn't really mean.

Thankfully, during the day, work kept her too busy to ponder her personal life. Word of their partnership was spreading. They had been besieged with media requests for interviews. Already a nice feature article had appeared in the Traverse City newspaper. The piece not only discussed Jaye's buy-in to the vineyard she'd helped begin, but Zack's decision to trade his stake in the venerable Holland Farms and gamble on a smaller and much newer Midwest operation.

The publicity was free and far-reaching. One such story ultimately was picked up by a wire service and made its way into wine columns and feature sections across the country. Zack's mother had even called to say she had read about their plans for Medallion in a publication there.

"We're creating buzz," he told Jaye.

Were they ever, and in local wine circles not all of it had to do with the vineyard. Despite their best efforts to be discreet, people were talking and speculating about the exact nature of the relationship between the two new partners. Corey was among them, even though she had a better understanding of what went on behind closed doors than most.

As she and Jaye chatted over coffee one Saturday afternoon in late November, apropos of nothing she mentioned, "I look good in most shades of blue."

Jaye stared at her blankly for a moment. "Sorry?"

"Blue. You know, for your bridesmaid dresses. No peach, please." Corey pulled a comical face. "It washes out my complexion."

"Ha, ha. Very funny." Jaye rolled her eyes and then sipped her coffee. The hand that held the cup wasn't quite steady, though.

"Actually, I'm serious, especially about my color preference."

"Corey, come on, you of all people know it's not like that between Zack and me."

But her friend was shaking her head even before Jaye finished speaking. "It's *exactly* like that. It's the Big *L*."

Love. The word hadn't even been said in its entirety and Jaye felt panicky. She choked down a mouthful of hot coffee. Outright denial seemed the best defense. "We're not falling for one another. We're just…" She shrugged.

"Just what? Having sex?"

"I was going to say having *incredible* sex, but yeah." Somehow Jaye managed to sound casual.

Corey wasn't put off. "So, you don't think you might be falling in love with him?"

"No. No!" she repeated a little more forcefully when her friend merely raised her eyebrows. "Zack and I like each other, sure, and we're compatible in many regards."

"Yes, I noticed that the other day when I walked into his office and he had his hands on your butt." Corey's tone was dry.

Jaye cleared her throat. "We try to keep it professional at work, but sometimes we become a little… affectionate."

"Honey, I'm a little affectionate with my cat. What you and Zack were getting ready to do in his office was—"

"What?" Jaye challenged.

"Well, let's just say after seeing the way the two of you look at each other I can understand why the polar ice cap is melting. It's the Big *L*," Corey announced for a second time.

Nerves tap-danced up Jaye's spine. "Oh, please. You're mistaking sexual chemistry for…for l-love." It was appalling, but she had a hard time getting out the word.

"I am not. I know all about sexual chemistry," Corey replied. "Even if it's been a while since I've actually experienced it firsthand with a man."

"Well then, you know it's a perfectly normal and healthy adult reaction that doesn't require a long-term commitment as a prerequisite. People have sex all the time without professing their undying devotion or making any plans to pick out china patterns."

"But I'm not talking about 'people,' Jaye. I'm talking about you and Zack. Your relationship goes well beyond sex."

"Of course it does." Jaye nodded matter-of-factly. "We own a business together."

"That's not what I'm talking about and you know it."
Corey's tone softened. "It's okay to admit you're scared."

"Scared? I'm not scared."

Corey merely continued. "Sure you are."

"Okay, fine." She crossed her arms. "Of what?"

"You're scared of getting hurt. You're scared of being
left or even that you might be the one to do the leaving,
like your mother did to your dad." She ticked off the
reasons with too much ease for Jaye's comfort.

"Corey, stop. I've heard enough."

But her friend wasn't through. "I think Zack is
scared, too, given what you told me happened with his
ex-fiancée."

"You're way off base," Jaye insisted.

"Well then, you're going to really take issue with
what I say next. Medallion is your dream, and I know
being in the vineyard makes you feel closer to your dad,
but I think the place is also your security blanket. You
love it the way you're afraid to love a man. You don't
trust people."

"Oh, please," she muttered, not liking in the least the
way Corey's summation nicked at old wounds.

"Zack's short on trust, too. You guys certainly don't
trust each other."

"I trust him," Jaye argued.

"Not with your heart, you don't."

Because it was true, Jaye evaded with, "My heart is
not an issue here."

"I don't buy that. Just like I don't buy your explanation that everything going on between the pair of you

is merely hormone-based. Why can't you just admit that maybe Zack is the one?"

Vulnerability turned her tone crisp. "There is no *one* for me. As for what's going on between us, it's not the Big *L,* Core, unless the *L* you're referring to stands for lust. Neither of us is looking for more than that."

Corey appeared both exasperated and sad. "Is that enough for you, honey?"

Jaye thought of the feelings both foreign and exciting that had her rolling over to reach for Zack long after he'd left her bed. "Let's just drop it, okay?"

"Okay." Corey sighed. "You don't need to answer that question for me. But do yourself a favor. Answer it for yourself."

As November passed into December, Zack and Jaye's days fell into a pleasant pattern. From sunrise until just after sunset, they worked side by side at the winery. She liked the fact that he had no qualms about tapping her superior knowledge of the area's climate and other factors that would affect the *terroir* of the wines they produced. In turn, she had no qualms about tapping his innate sense of style when it came to outfitting the inn. Renovations of a couple of the bedrooms were under way, with work crews adding a new full bath for one. The addition of Zack's living quarters just off the main floor would take more time, but the footings for the foundation had been poured.

In the evenings Jaye and Zack holed up in the kitchen, going over material swatches and paint chips and thumbing through the furniture catalogues the interior designer they'd hired had provided. Where Jaye would have played it safe with neutral color choices for bed comforters and window treatments, Zack and the designer were opting for drama and a far more opulent color palette.

"We make wine," Zack said in explaining why the vivid color choices appealed to him. "Why shouldn't we bring the greens, burgundies and other hues found out in the vineyard indoors?"

So, this evening, as the construction crew that was installing the new upstairs bathroom banged away, Zack and Jaye sat at the island in the kitchen and made the final selections from the choices spread out in front of them.

"Which color do you propose for the walls in Suite One?" She held her breath half expecting him to pluck one of the deeper-hued paint chips from the pile.

But he reached for the bottle of wine they'd had with dinner and levered out the cork. "How about this?"

"That's a cork, not a color."

"But the people at the paint store can match anything these days thanks to computers. It's a nice neutral shade that will complement the darker-hued accessories we've selected."

Jaye tried to picture it but couldn't. She shrugged, "You're the expert."

"No, Diane's the expert," he said, referring to the decorator. "We'll run it by her to see if she agrees."

"The pair of you have been in sync on everything so far. I think she might have a crush on you."

He grinned. "Jealous?"

"Not as long as she keeps her hands to herself." Jaye's tone was teasing, but she wasn't sure she was. She opted to get back to business. "So, what about the floors? What should we do with them?"

"Diane and I think rich, dark wood with plush area rugs the color of champagne."

"Mmm. Sounds decadent."

"Very." He leaned over to trace the line of her jaw with his fingertips, and she swore her blood began to bubble and fizz like sparkling wine. "They'll be so soft our guests won't want to sleep on the beds."

"Who says they'll be sleeping at all? This place will be far too romantic to waste time slumbering."

"Romantic?"

"Very." Jaye made a little humming noise. "You know, that's how we should market it."

"As a couple's getaway?" he asked. "A place where a man and a woman can retreat from reality and concentrate on their most basic needs?"

The passion simmering in his eyes made it impossible to speak, so Jaye nodded.

"What do you find romantic?" He stroked her face again, his caress featherlight and full of promise. "What makes you go all soft inside?"

Before she could think better of it, Jaye whispered, "You."

Zack was the one struck mute this time. Her reply touched him on a level he hadn't expected—an emotional level that was much trickier to navigate than a purely physical one. He reached for her hand and brought it to his mouth for a kiss. Then he used it to tug Jaye out of her chair.

"Come here." He pulled her toward him until she stood between the vee of his thighs. His kiss was hot, urgent and it made his desire plain.

"I see I have the opposite effect on you," she murmured with a throaty laugh when he stood and pulled her flush against him. Indeed, there was nothing soft about his body at the moment.

"This seems to happen whenever we're together."

"So I've noticed."

"I take it you don't mind," he said on a grin.

"Not in the least."

Jaye gathered her hair to one side, allowing him greater access to her neck, which he nuzzled on his way down to her collarbone. When he ran into the fabric of her blouse he unfastened the first button.

She glanced toward the door. Anyone could just walk right in. "M-maybe we should take this someplace a little more private.

In answer Zack lifted her up until her hips were perched on the island's granite surface. The move brought her breasts nearly level with his mouth. She forgot all about modesty when he went back to what he'd been doing.

Jaye shivered visibly as the second, third and fourth buttons of her blouse gave way. Zack parted the fabric to reveal the perfection beneath it, and with reverent hands stroked the pale exposed skin. When his fingers found the front clasp to her bra he heard her breath hitch. When he nudged the lace aside, she shuddered. When he lowered her head to savor her sweetness, she moaned low and long.

"Zack, I love…" For one mind-blowing moment he thought she was going to say she loved him, but she finished with "…the way you make me feel."

"Like this you mean?" he asked. He lowered his head again and her control snapped completely, as evidenced by the way she wrapped her long legs around his waist and arched her back. Her fingers were fisted in his hair, holding on, holding him close.

"Yes," she murmured. "Please."

What blood remained in his head took a quick detour south. The hard surface of the island beckoned. In his desperation it looked as soft and inviting as a down-filled mattress. Even the floor's cool travertine tiles held potential as Zack levered away from Jaye's straining body and struggled with the snap of her jeans.

Over the roaring in his ears and their combined labored breathing, the sound of work boots thudding down the stairs somehow managed to register. Jaye stopped, stiffened, as she apparently heard them, too. As the sound's meaning dawned, she quickly extricated her legs from around Zack's waist and hopped down. She managed to get her bra refastened as well as a couple of her blouse's buttons done before the door swung open and the work crew supervisor entered the kitchen.

The man glanced between the pair of them. Jaye's

face was flushed, her neck mottled from its encounter with Zack's late-day stubble. As for Zack, he was grateful for the high counter that hid the more incriminating evidence of his arousal, although nothing could camouflage the fact that he was breathing as if he'd just run a marathon.

"I...I...probably should have knocked," the man said.

"Nah. No need. Jaye and I were just...we were just picking out paint colors for the bedrooms," Zack said. Too late he realized that the samples were scattered all over the floor like confetti.

The work supervisor eyed them for a moment before clearing his throat. "Well, I wanted to let you know we're done for the day."

Zack bobbed his head. "Fine."

"The plumber got the piping installed on the new upstairs bath, and the wiring is finished, too. Once everything passes inspection the drywall will go up. I'm shooting for end of next week on that, although it may get done sooner."

"Terrific," Jaye managed.

"Yeah, thanks for the update," Zack said.

"No problem." The supervisor's lips twitched when he added, "You two have a good night."

When he was gone, Jaye and Zack eyed one another from opposite sides of the island.

"That guy has lousy timing," Zack muttered.

"The worst," she agreed. She motioned to the flat surface in front of her. "Another minute and..."

Zack snorted. "Exactly."

They heard the clatter of more work boots and then the front door closed. They were alone in the house now. There would be no further interruptions. Zack didn't move, though. The urgent heat of a moment ago had cooled. Now something more consuming than sex weighed on his mind.

I love...

In the brief moment before Jaye had finished that sentence, he'd experienced myriad emotions, some more troubling than others. Afterward, he'd been confused, because he'd felt oddly disappointed with her words. He needed to think.

"I should be going, too," he said slowly.

A couple weeks earlier he'd moved his belongings out of one of the spare rooms, taking up lodgings at a bed-and-breakfast in Sutton's Bay instead. Even the new couch in the break room had become too damned uncomfortable. Jaye had offered to be the one to relocate. As she'd pointed out, the house was more his than hers but Zack had been living out of suitcases for a few months now. He hadn't grown used to it exactly, but he had enough chivalry not to displace her until the addition of his quarters to the main level of the house was complete. In the meantime, she'd hooked up with a real estate agent and was looking for a new place.

Of course, one of the reasons he'd relocated was to keep the construction crew, which consisted of local craftsmen, from talking. It was a good bet they would be now.

A less comfortable truth was that while he wanted to move into the house, he didn't want Jaye to move out.

He liked, a little too much, the idea of both of them under one roof throughout the long, winter nights.

His evolving feelings for Jaye worried him. In the beginning those feelings had been based almost exclusively on sexual attraction. He'd wanted her and she'd desired him right back. Thus the no-strings arrangement they'd agreed upon at the outset had been simple and safe. Then, a few minutes earlier, when he thought Jaye might be getting ready to say she loved him, he'd been forced to confront his concerns head-on: What if their relationship went beyond sex? What if it was the beginning of something bigger?

Then, when she hadn't said the words, a different set of concerns had arisen: What if he discovered he wanted far more from Jaye than she'd already made clear she was capable of giving or interested in having? Worse, what if when it was all said and done Zack once again discovered that his main attraction for a woman was the land he owned?

He didn't like the answers he came up with to any of those hypothetical questions, so when Jaye said, "It's snowing outside. The roads might be slippery. You... you could stay the night," he shook his head.

"I think it's best I go."

Tugging at the ends of her hair, she asked, "Why?"

"It's hard to explain." He scrubbed a hand over his face. "I...I just don't think it's a good idea for me to stay here."

"Tonight? Or any night?"

"I don't know. Sorry. I'm not making much sense."

Jaye nibbled her lower lip. "Scared?"

It was an odd question and Zack wasn't completely sure what she meant by it. Even so, he didn't ask for clarification. "Half to death."

As he grabbed his coat and headed for the door, he thought he heard her reply, "I am, too."

CHAPTER NINE

JAYE lay awake long into the night feeling lonely, feeling confused. God help her, she'd almost done it. She'd almost blurted out, "I love you" while she and Zack had been tearing at each other's clothing in the kitchen. She wanted to blame the near declaration on sex, as she had in the past, but she'd be lying. Laying a shaky hand over her thumping heart, she admitted the truth to herself at last.

She loved Zack.

Earlier, in the kitchen, she thought she'd covered her tracks well enough, but his hasty retreat after the construction supervisor's unfortunate interruption had her rethinking that assessment.

And that was why she couldn't sleep.

Zack hadn't looked too pleased about the possibility that her emotions might be more binding than the no-strings sort she'd professed entering into their relationship.

In truth, Jaye wasn't particularly pleased, either.

Scared?

She blamed Corey for planting the question in her

subconscious. The fact that it had slipped out wasn't nearly as disconcerting as Zack's response: *Half to death.*

Was that a good thing or a bad thing? In the end Jaye decided she wasn't ready to find out. Before drifting off to sleep at last, she convinced herself she was perfectly content with the status quo.

As Christmas approached, however, the status quo took another hit. Their quasi-couplehood proved awkward with the holiday season looming. They'd made it through Thanksgiving without too much fuss. Zack had stayed in Sutton's Bay. But then, flying to California for what amounted to a long weekend probably hadn't been all that appealing. They'd spent the day together, shared a not-so-traditional meal of lasagna, since the housekeeper had the day off, and other than pizza Jaye couldn't cook much else.

But Christmas was different. Jaye had no immediate family to spend the day with. Zack did. Strained though his relationship with his family might be, this was the time of year to put grievances aside and gather with loved ones.

By the second week of December, though, he still had not mentioned anything about going to California. Nor had he said anything about staying in Michigan. Jaye was dying to know his plans, but she didn't ask. As with so much else in their relationship, she opted to wait, wonder…and pretend the outcome was really of no consequence to her.

Finally the suspense ended.

"My mother called this afternoon," Zack mentioned as they ate dinner in the kitchen a week before Christmas.

The housekeeper had prepared the meal and then left the salad chilling in the fridge and the main course warming in the oven before going home for the day. All Jaye had done was set the table. Zack had poured the wine.

"Oh? Everything okay?" She had to raise her voice to be heard over the hammering coming from the back of the house. The construction crew was working late to frame the addition, since this would be the last week they worked until after the holidays.

"Everything's fine." He cleared his throat then. "She asked me to come home for Christmas."

The dried cherries in the salad turned sour in Jaye's mouth. Still, she worked up a smile. "That's nice. I can drive you to the airport if you'd like, save you the hassle of long-term parking. When will you be leaving?"

He studied her a moment. Then he said, "Actually, I haven't decided if I'm going."

Her spirits rose ridiculously. "Oh?"

"I probably should."

"Yes." She tried to sound sincere. "It is Christmas."

He pushed chunks of romaine lettuce around on his plate with the tines of his fork. "I know, and I wasn't there last year, a fact that my mother reminded me of today."

"Where did you go last year?" Jaye was too curious to wonder if it was any of her business.

One side of his mouth lifted as he glanced up. "Well, when I wasn't looking at vineyards to buy I was wallowing in self-pity on the ski slopes in Aspen. I spent the bulk of December at a friend's chalet waiting for my father to call, tell me I was right about the direction I wanted for Holland Farms and beg me to return. Obviously, that didn't happen."

"Holland's loss is Medallion's gain."

His laughter rumbled. "Bet you didn't think you'd be saying that when I first got here."

"Not then. No," she agreed. "But I mean it. Medallion already produced a quality product before you bought it, but now…" She shook her head in wonder and smiled fully. "This vineyard is on track to become everything my father and I always hoped it would be. I couldn't have done any of it alone."

Her heartfelt comments didn't seem to please him. In fact, he frowned. "Good to know I could be of use to you."

"Zack?"

He waved a hand. "Forget it. I'm not in the best mood. And the phone call from my mom didn't help." He shook his head. "She sent me on quite the guilt trip."

"I'm sure that's only because she misses you."

Jaye thought of her own mother. It would be nice to be missed. She hadn't heard from Heather in years, unless one counted the sympathy card she'd sent Jaye after Frank's death. Her mother had signed it with her first name only. Beneath the typed sentiment, she hadn't included a more personal note. Jaye's insurance agent had at least penned the standard, "thinking of you."

"I know she misses me, which is why I feel so lousy." He set his fork down, pushed his plate to one side.

Because he looked so miserable, she found it easy to say, "Go home for Christmas."

"Is that what you want?" he asked softly.

"Of course." She kept her tone upbeat and her smile bright. "What else would I want? Besides, the longer you put off going back for a visit the more awkward it's going to be to see everyone when you finally do."

"I'm not worried about it being awkward. Sure, I'm still ticked off about my father always taking Phillip's side in everything, and I'm not exactly thrilled my cousin hooked up with my ex, but I'm over all that. I'm long over Mira."

"I didn't mean to suggest otherwise," she replied.

Still, his words had Jaye's heart lifting. Sometimes she'd wondered…okay, maybe even worried. She'd come across a picture of the other woman in a growers trade publication that had done a feature story on Holland Farms. Mira was gorgeous, petite and ultra-feminine. In other words, she was everything that Jaye was not. Jaye hadn't cared at all for the stab of envy she'd felt any more than she'd appreciated the self-doubts that had ensued.

He didn't appear mollified. "I wouldn't be with one woman and pine for another, Jaye. That's not my style."

"Good to know. Just for the record, though, I didn't say that you were." She plucked up her napkin and fussed with it for a moment before repositioning it on her lap. "Still, you can be over someone and not be over what they did to you."

"Well, you'd know."

"What do you mean by that?"

He waved one hand, picked up his fork. "Forget it."

"No. What do you think I'm not over?" she asked.

He set the fork aside again. "Your mother's desertion."

His reply was so unexpected that Jaye's head snapped back as if she'd taken an unexpected jab to the chin. "Wh-what?"

"You heard me. She left when you were what...? Twelve?"

"Almost thirteen."

"A kid, but as far as I can tell, you've used the fact that she walked out on you and your father as the reason not to trust long-term relationships."

"That's not true." But it was. Hadn't Corey said the very same thing? And Corey had known Jaye for ages. After a matter of months Zack had pegged her exactly. Jaye didn't like how easily he'd accomplished that, so she shifted gears. "Besides, we're not talking about me."

"No, we're not, and isn't that handy? You've got some issues to deal with yourself."

"I don't have *issues*. And my mother has nothing to do with my relationships with men," she snapped. But she couldn't maintain eye contact.

"Liar. You all but said so yourself."

"When?" Her gaze collided with his again. Surely she'd never confided such a thing.

"Before we became involved. I recall very clearly you telling me that you weren't interested in marrying anyone."

She hadn't been…then. But now? Because she was feeling vulnerable, she tipped up her chin. "Yeah. So?"

"I've never met a woman yet who didn't want to hear the wedding march."

"Well, now you have," she bluffed.

"Why? Got *issues,* Jaye?" he asked softly.

Eager to steer the conversation in a different direction, she turned the question back around. "Why aren't *you* interested in a serious relationship?"

"Who says I'm not?"

"You are?" She blinked. Her heart rose again, lurching into her throat.

"Eventually, sure." He shrugged. "Unlike you, I haven't ruled one out completely." He seemed angry suddenly. "Unlike you, this damned vineyard isn't the be-all, end-all for me. Ultimately I want more from life than to have Medallion toasted in wine circles. When both the timing and the woman are right, I have no doubt I'll want to settle down and start a family."

Forget feeling sucker punched. Jaye felt as if she'd been KO-ed. Through a haze of emotions she could almost picture a referee standing over her counting.

"Well, glad I can help you kill time until then." Somehow she managed to sound wry rather than wrecked.

Zack grimaced, apparently realizing how utterly insulting his words had sounded. "God, Jaye, I'm sorry. That came out all wrong."

"No, no." She waved a hand. "You have no reason to apologize. We're both well aware of—" she swallowed before continuing "—the limitations of our relationship."

"Yeah. Right. The limitations. I guess I thought…" His words trailed off.

"What did you think?"

But he shook his head. "Forget it. It doesn't matter." He snatched the napkin off his lap and tossed it aside. As he rose to his feet, he said, "There's some paperwork back at the office I need to go over."

"But you haven't finished dinner."

"I'm not really hungry right now. I'll see you in the morning."

After he'd gone, Jaye had no appetite either. She threw the baked chicken breasts and herbed rice into the garbage and then set the dirty dishes in the sink.

As the first tear leaked down her cheek, she murmured, "What a waste." But she knew it wasn't the ruined meal that was making her cry.

Zack hadn't slept well. Hell, he hadn't slept at all. Ever since his dinner with Jaye, emotions had been bubbling, as uncontrollable and potentially dangerous as a volcano's eruption.

Something, he knew, was going to give.

When he arrived at Medallion's offices just after dawn the next morning, Jaye was already at her desk. She glanced up when he stopped at her door. Her eyes looked shadowed and her demeanor was reserved. She was winding one long cinnamon curl around her index finger. She always fussed with her hair when she was nervous or distressed. It was a small comfort to know she'd passed as miserable a night as he had.

"Good morning," he said.

"Morning."

He pointed to the cup on her blotter. "Need a refill when I go for coffee?"

"No, I'm good. Thanks."

Zack shifted his stance so he could tuck his hands into the front pockets of his pants. "Look, Jaye, I feel horrible about last night."

"There's no reason to. What you said was only the truth." She coiled the hair so tightly that the tip of her finger turned purple.

"It wasn't remotely close to the truth." That was what had kept him awake half the night. So, once again he opted to come clean. "You're much more important to me than I made it sound with my thoughtless remark. I'm not just killing time, as you put it. It goes deeper— much deeper—than that."

She uncoiled the curl. Her voice was a hoarse whisper. "For me, too."

He sighed and leaned against the doorjamb. "So, what are we going to do about those limitations, Jaye?"

She wound another curl around her finger. "I don't know. I want…I want…" Her lips compressed and shook her head.

It shouldn't be that hard to say, but then he'd hardly put his own thoughts into words. "It looks like we both have some thinking to do." He cleared his throat. "I've decided to fly home for Christmas."

Her eyes widened. For a moment he thought he glimpsed disappointment. But then she smiled. "Good.

I mean, you should spend the day with loved ones. Have you called your mother yet to tell her?"

"Last night. From the way she carried on I think she's planning to slay a fatted calf or something." He laughed.

"Nah." Jaye shook her head. "They only do that for prodigal sons. You weren't acting reckless by leaving. You had a very good reason. Just as now you have a good reason to go home."

She'd helped him see that, he realized. "So what are your plans for Christmas?"

"I don't really have any." She shrugged. "I'll probably have dinner at Corey's. I've got an open invitation there."

The answer wasn't what he'd hoped to hear. "What about...family? You have relatives downstate."

"My aunt asked me if I'd like to come for a few days, but I declined. It's not like we're super close or anything." She glanced toward the window. "Besides, there's plenty to keep me occupied with the house renovations and decorating."

"Jaye—"

But she cut him off. "If we plan to open the inn by the end of May to take advantage of the Memorial Day weekend crowds, we've got to get going on publicity. Mindy has been working on a press release and media kit," she said, referring to their marketing director. "She said she'd have the materials to me by the twenty-second of the month, the twenty-third at the latest. I'll go over everything, make any necessary changes, so that we can have them mailed out before the first of the year."

"You don't need to work through the holidays."

"I know I don't *need* to. I want to. Really." Then she admitted, "It will keep my mind off my dad."

It was her first Christmas without him. For a moment Zack contemplated asking her to come to California with him. They could stretch out their visit through the first of the year, tour Napa Valley and sample the competition's offerings. He could introduce her to his parents. The idea smacked squarely into those "limitations" they were supposed to be weighing.

"Well, I'll only be gone a few days," he told her.

Zack booked his flight, made his plans, all with a heavy heart. He needed to go home. His mother was expecting him and it was time to face his father, his cousin and Mira. But he didn't want to leave Jaye. So much between them was…unresolved. Of course, neither one of them was willing to make the first move. Maybe they'd never be ready.

Jaye drove him to the airport on Christmas Eve morning, keeping the conversation light on the way into Traverse City. He was due to return four days later. That seemed a lifetime away. When she parked the car, Zack stopped her before she open her door.

"I have something for you. I was going to leave it under your tree."

"I didn't put up a tree," she said.

"I know. That's why I brought it with me and decided to give it to you now."

"Do I have to wait till morning to open it?" He liked

the eagerness he heard in her tone and the excitement that brimmed in her eyes. Both had been lacking in recent days. Her father's loss weighed heavily on her, he knew. It was small of him, but Zack also hoped she was going to miss him, too.

"Nah. You can open it now." He pulled the small gift-wrapped box from his pocket and handed it to her. "You're a hard woman to buy for, by the way."

"You didn't have to get me anything." But she was gleefully shredding the paper as she said it. Then she lifted the lid on the box and gasped. "Oh, my God."

Her stunned reaction had Zack smiling, but just to be sure, he asked, "So, do you like it?"

"I love it." She lifted the silver necklace from the box and inspected the pendant. It was a small cluster of grape-shaped amethyst stones—an exact replica of the fruit that adorned Medallion's label.

"I know you don't wear much jewelry, but I thought you might make an exception for this. I had it custom-made by an artisan my mother recommended. I know how much you love Medallion. This way it will always be close to your heart."

"It's gorgeous. Perfect." Her eyes grew bright.

"Jaye?"

"Sorry." She blinked away the unshed tears. "It's a very thoughtful gift, Zack. I can't remember the last time someone gave me something so beautiful."

"Let me put it on you," he suggested.

She lifted her hair so he could reach behind her

neck and fasten the clasp. The pendant rested just above her breasts.

"It looks good enough to eat," he said, bobbing his eyebrows in an effort to lighten the moment.

Jaye leaned over to kiss him. Afterward, she said, "Medallion's not the only thing dear to my heart, Zack."

"Oh?" His pulse beat unsteadily. He thought he knew what she was saying, but he needed to know for sure. "And?"

"I'm not good with words," she murmured, lowering her head and sighing. "I'm not good at a lot of things when it comes to expressing my feelings."

"You're doing fine."

But she shook her head. "I put something in your luggage."

"A Christmas present?"

"In a way. And an explanation of sorts."

"I'm not sure I understand."

"You will. And if it's…it's not to your liking, well, you can return it and…" She motioned with her hand. "I'll be okay with that. I'll understand."

She wasn't making any sense. "Jaye—"

But she'd opened her door and was getting out of the car. "Come on. We'd better hurry or you'll miss your flight."

CHAPTER TEN

THE first thing Zack noticed when he arrived at his family's vineyard was how much warmer the weather was. In Michigan the temperature had been hovering in the teens for weeks. Here, it was a balmy fifty-eight. He took a moment to savor that and the familiar scents and sounds after he parked his rental car and walked to the house.

His mother was out the door before he reached the front steps. Judith Holland's eyes crinkled with delight as she bounded down the stairs and called his name. Zack dropped his bag and scooped her into his arms for a hug, resting his chin on the crown of her head as they swayed back and forth in the drive. God, he'd missed her.

"Hi, Mom," he said when the embrace ended.

She sniffed and knuckled away a tear. "You're a sight for sore eyes."

"Same here."

Zack grabbed his bag and looped his free arm around her shoulders. When they started for the house, he realized his father was standing on the porch. Ross

Holland's emotions were far less obvious and more difficult to read than Judith's had been. But he shook Zack's hand, held open the door and inquired politely, "How was your flight, son?"

The question seemed to be an olive branch of sorts. Zack decided to accept it.

"The airports were a zoo, but my flight was fine. It's good to see you, Dad."

"Why don't we go inside?" Zack's mother suggested. Her smile bright, her gaze full of hope. "We can catch up over coffee."

"Or a glass of wine." His father rested a hand on Zack's shoulder. "I bet Zack wouldn't mind tasting last year's barrel-aged chardonnay."

"Did it turn out well, then?"

"Better than well. You were right about the Hungarian oak." Another olive branch.

"Thank you."

Ross nodded. "I think it will be hard to beat in tasting competitions this year."

"Don't go counting your gold medals just yet," Zack replied with a grin. "Medallion has something pretty special for the judges to try, too."

Later that evening as they sat in the den, sampling a nice Sangiovese, talking shop and watching the flames in the fireplace flicker and dance, his father surprised him by saying, "I want you to come back."

Zack straightened in his chair, not sure he'd heard correctly. "Back to California?"

His father nodded. "Back to Holland Farms. This is

where you belong." Hearing those words meant the world to Zack, until his dad added, "Phillip and I have been giving your inn proposal some more thought."

"So this is Phillip's idea, asking me to return." Even though his cousin wasn't in the room, Zack felt his presence and resented it. Nothing had changed. Zack was still the odd man out. For some reason that no longer bothered him quite as much as it once had.

"It's not Phillip's idea," his father insisted. "It's mine." Zack's surprise must have been obvious, because his father shook his head in dismay. "I can see that you don't quite believe me."

"It's not a question of believing you. Let's just say prior experience has given me reason to doubt that what I have to contribute will be taken seriously around here."

"I know that's been the case in the past." Ross studied his wine. "I'm sorry about that. I'm not very good at accepting change. You always seemed to want to shake things up."

"But for good reason," Zack protested. "There's nothing wrong with keeping certain things the same. In fact, I'd be the first one to decry change for the sake of change. But you and Phillip vetoed every idea I offered to improve the Holland brand's name recognition with consumers."

"I know it seemed that way."

"It *was* that way, Dad."

He expected Ross to argue, but the older man didn't. Instead, his father seemed to change the subject. "Your mother really misses you."

Zack sighed. "I know. I'll…I'll try to get back more often once things settle down at Medallion." He'd already told his father about the luxury bed-and-breakfast they would be opening in the spring, and so he added, "You and Mom are always welcome to come out and see me. The inn will be ready for guests by the end of May." He winked. "I'll set you up in the honeymoon suite."

Ross chuckled. "Your mother would love that."

"The package includes complimentary sparkling wine and gourmet breakfast that can be served in the room."

"Sounds like you've thought of everything."

"I had a little help," Zack replied, thinking of Jaye. Missing her.

"So, you won't consider returning? Holland needs you. I need you."

He'd waited a lifetime to hear his father say that. Since selling his stake in Holland, he'd fantasized about just this scenario. But Zack shook his head. Someone needed him at Medallion, too. And he needed that someone right back. He loved Jaye. It was time he admitted that, not only to himself but to the woman in question.

Jaye was on his mind when he went up to his old room an hour later. He considered calling her, but the time difference had him hanging up before dialing. In the morning he'd phone. He wanted to hear her voice. He hadn't unpacked yet, so he hefted his suitcase onto the bed and unzipped it. That's when he spied Jaye's gift.

He ripped away the festive wrapping paper and frowned at the Greek fisherman's cap. The crown was faded, its felt lining worn. Why on earth would she give him this? Then he read the note and his heart lifted. The last of his doubts about her feelings and their future fell away.

Don't worry, I don't expect you to wear this. It was my dad's. He wore it each spring when he went to inspect the vineyard after the last frost of the season. He called it his good-luck charm, and I figure there must be something to it since Medallion's vines always seemed to make it through the harsh winters intact.

Anyway, I wanted you to have it. In a lot of ways, you're just like my dad: solid, dependable. Someone I can trust.

Solid. Dependable. Trustworthy. Some men might prefer the woman they were dating to use more exciting adjectives to describe them. To Zack, though, these were perfect and significant. Her relationships with men had been stunted by her mother's desertion. She was letting Zack know she trusted him as much as she'd trusted her father. She was letting Zack know she now trusted herself.

She finished the note with this telling play on words: "There's no *limit* to my feelings for you. See you soon. Love, Jaye."

Long before the sun came up the next morning, Zack was dressed and in the kitchen. His mother smiled when she came through the door wearing her robe.

"You always were the first out of bed on Christmas," she teased, walking over to give him a kiss on the cheek.

"The only difference now is that instead of sniffing around under the tree, shaking my gifts and trying to guess their contents, I brewed a pot of coffee."

"So I see." She poured her cup. After she'd sipped it, she said, "I'm grateful for the coffee, but I miss that eager little boy. It's not fair that children grow up so quickly and leave home."

Zack cleared his throat. "Speaking of leaving, I…I changed my flight plans. I need to get back, Mom. Today."

Her face fell and she protested, "Oh, no. Not today, Zack. It's Christmas. What's so important in Michigan that you need to fly out today?"

"It's not what. Actually, it's who."

"Oh?" Her brows rose.

"There's this woman, Mom," he began.

She was grinning long before Zack finished.

Jaye dined with Corey and her family, but begged off early even though her friend had asked her to stay. By eight she was wearing a pair of silk pajamas and curled up beneath the comforter on her bed watching television and trying to pretend she wasn't waiting for the phone to ring.

She hadn't heard from Zack since he'd left. It had only been one day, she reminded herself. Still, she felt as if he'd been gone a lifetime. She glanced at the clock. It was five in the afternoon California time. Zack was probably eating dinner with his family. Jaye's lips puckered. And Mira. She ran her fingers over the pendant on the necklace he'd given her and wondered what he thought of the gift she'd given him. Maybe he hadn't understood its meaning. Maybe he had and didn't know how to react to her bald admission that her feelings had no limit when it came to him. Maybe his luggage had been lost.

"Maybe I'm being an idiot," she muttered aloud.

Only a couple more days and he would be back. Then she wouldn't have to speculate. She'd know.

When the doorbell peeled a moment later, she was tempted to ignore it. She wasn't dressed for company, nor was she in the mood to entertain. Most likely, though, it was Corey, who would no doubt try to talk Jaye into coming back over. If she didn't answer the door, her friend would stand out there all night, ringing the bell and worrying. She pulled on a robe and headed downstairs.

"I'm not in the mood for more visiting," she announced as she opened the door. Then her mouth dropped open. Zack stood on the porch. He was wearing her father's battered cap. Its black brim pulled low over his forehead. His longish hair flowed out from underneath it at the back. He looked ridiculous. He looked utterly perfect.

"What are you in the mood for?" he asked with a grin.

"I...I..."

"I love it when you're tongue-tied." He winked. "For some reason I find it incredibly sexy."

"Wh-what are you doing here?" she finally managed.

"I thought that would be obvious." His jaunty demeanor ebbed. Zack took off the cap and held it in his hands in front of him. "I don't know that I've ever received a gift quite like this one."

"A lot of thought went into it. It didn't cost as much as the necklace you gave me, but—"

Zack stopped her. "It's far more valuable than that necklace, Jaye."

"I can't believe you're here."

"I had to see you."

"Yeah?"

"When a woman tells you there's no limit to her feelings, well, a smart man catches the first flight out."

Her smile bloomed, trembled. "Is that what you did?"

"I'm here, aren't I?"

He stepped over the threshold and kicked the door closed behind him as he reached for her. Jaye's emotions reeled and her pulse sped up, making her hands shake when she laid them on his chest. Beneath her fingers she could feel his heart beating as furiously as her own.

Joy bubbled through her with the effervescence of champagne. "But you're supposed to be in California spending today with loved ones."

His kiss was tender. His words melted his heart. "That's what I'm doing, Jaye. I love you."

EPILOGUE

SPRING was always a magical time at Medallion. This year it was especially so. Not only was another growing season at hand, another season of Jaye's life had started. She felt reborn right along with the vines that had begun to sprout leaves now that the weather was turning warmer and the days were stretching longer.

Since Christmas, when Zack had arrived on her doorstep professing his love and wearing the cap she'd given him as a symbol of her trust, Jaye had discovered that in sharing herself completely with this man, she felt whole for the first time in years.

They hadn't talked about marriage, but it was the next logical step, one she was no longer skeptical about taking. She didn't just trust Zack. She trusted herself. She wasn't like her mother. She wouldn't wake up one morning and decide she'd had enough of playing house or raising a child. Zack was the person she saw herself waking up next to for the rest of her life. Like her dad had been, Jaye was the sort who took her commitments seriously.

In the meantime they had a wedding to attend. Phillip and Mira's. Jaye decided to wear the sexy red dress Corey had given her before the harvest party. She had the confidence to wear it now. She didn't mind attracting attention, as long as the attention she attracted was Zack's.

She and Zack arrived in California the day before the nuptials were to take place. Jaye had known that Holland Farms was a much larger operation, but it wasn't until she saw it firsthand that she understood the vast scope of Zack's family's vineyard. It was massive in comparison to Medallion, with five times the acreage, three times the staff, and of course it enjoyed a much longer and richer history.

He could be part of it again. All he had to do was say the word and his stake in Holland would be restored. He'd told her that himself after Christmas. Just as he'd told her how much it meant to hear his father say, "I need you."

"I can't recall him ever using those words," he'd said, sounding a bit awed.

Twice since then his father had made the pitch for him to return, sweetening the deal a little more each time. Zack steadfastly refused, but now that she was at Holland, Jaye felt the first twinges of regret. Maybe this was where he belonged, especially now that he could have a real say in the operation.

They were just leaving for the church, driving past the seemingly endless rows of vines, when Jaye reached her decision.

"Stop. Stop the car," she told him.

Zack pulled the rented sports coupe to the side of the road. Its tires spat gravel in his haste.

"What's wrong? Are you okay?"

"I'm fine. I just needed to tell you something."

He glanced at his watch. "Right now, Jaye? The wedding starts in less than half an hour."

"I know it does. I'm sorry. But, yes, I need to say this right now." Her tone was urgent, matching her feelings.

"Okay," he said slowly.

Jaye unbuckled her seat belt and got out of the car.

"Hey, where are you going?" he called, switching off the ignition and doing the same.

She didn't reply. Instead, she motioned with one arm for him to follow her and crossed into the vineyard, unmindful of the way her heels sank into the soil. Once there, she stood between two rows of trellised vines, put her arms out and turned in a semicircle.

When she was facing him again, she smiled. "This place is incredible, Zack."

He put his hands on his hips and eyed her as if she'd gone mad. "That's what you wanted to tell me?"

"Yes. I mean, no." She shook her head, trying to think of the best way to put her thoughts into words.

He tapped the face of his watch. "Jaye, we're going to be late."

"I know. Bear with me, please." Then she plowed ahead. "When we first met you told me that vineyards are just soil and vines. Pieces of real estate that represent more of an investment than anything else."

He frowned. "Yeah, I said that."

"And you believed it?"

"At the time," he admitted.

"Do you still believe it?" she demanded.

"No." Zack wasn't sure where she was going with this conversation, but Jaye had changed his mind about that. She'd changed his mind about a lot of things.

"I didn't think so." She appeared both relieved and sad.

"Jaye?"

But she shook her head. "I know I'm not making much sense, but humor me a minute longer, okay?"

"Sure."

"If my mom came back next week. If she just showed up on my doorstep, what do you think I should do?"

"Has she contacted you?"

"No. I'm just asking your opinion."

He rubbed the back of his neck. "I'd guess I'd encourage you to listen to what she had to say."

"If she wanted me to be part of her life again, and if she wanted to be part of mine, would you encourage that?"

"Sure, Jaye."

"Because family is important."

"Exactly."

She nodded. "And because you love me."

"I think you're acting a little nutty right now, but yes, I love you."

"And because you love me, you'd do what you could to make me happy. You'd make sacrifices for me."

He stepped closer, reached for her arms. "I'd move heaven and earth for you," he said simply.

Her eyes filled with tears even as she smiled. "I think you should sell Medallion."

Zack took a step back, sure he'd misheard her. But she was saying, "A buyer would be easy to find."

His blood ran cold at the statement. Old doubts bubbled to the surface. "You?" he asked quietly.

"No." She shook her head sending cinnamon-colored curls dancing. "I don't want to buy you out. I'm going to sell my share, too."

He blinked. "Jaye, honey, you've lost me. Why would you sell? Medallion means everything to you."

"No. I thought it did, but I was wrong. *You* mean everything to me, Zack. I can be happy living anywhere. Well, as long as it's at a vineyard and as long as I'm with you."

"What exactly are you saying?"

"Your father wants you to return to Holland Farms. Your mother misses you terribly. This place, it's been in your family for generations. You belong here."

He nodded, even though he didn't agree. "So, you'd sell Medallion, you'd trade in your dream, so that I could come back here, reclaim my birthright, so to speak."

She swallowed, but that was the only sign she gave of regret. "Yes."

If Zack hadn't loved her insanely already, he would have then. "But you once told me that Medallion was your life?"

She stepped closer and framed his face with her hands. "Turns out I was wrong, Zackary Holland. You're my life."

There was only one way to respond to a declaration like that. And so when he finished kissing her, he got down on one knee.

"You're my life, too, Jaye. You know I love you. I love Medallion, too. It's not just soil or real estate. But it is an investment and a dream. One I want to share with you."

"But Holland—"

"Is my past," he finished. "I'm more interested in looking ahead. Will you marry me?"

She was laughing and crying at the same time. When he reached out to wipe away her tear, she said, "Most definitely."

They didn't make it to his cousin's wedding. They did manage to put in an appearance at the reception hall, arriving just in time for the best man's toast to the bride and groom.

A smiling Zack and Jaye raised their glasses with the rest of the guests, but the future they drank to was their own.

* * * * *

Love Inspired
HISTORICAL

Powerful, engaging stories of romance,
adventure and faith
set in the past—when life was simpler and faith
played a major role in everyday lives.

Turn the page for a sneak preview of
THE BRITON
by
Catherine Palmer

Love Inspired Historical—love and faith
throughout the ages
A brand-new line from Steeple Hill Books
Launching this February!

"Welcome to the family, Briton," said one of Olaf's men in a mocking voice. "We look forward to the presence of a woman at our hall."

Bronwen grasped her tunic and yanked it from the Viking's thick fingers. As she stepped away from the table, she heard the drunken laughter of the barbarians behind her. How could her father have betrothed her to the old Viking?

Running down the stone steps toward the heavy oak door that led outside from the keep, Bronwen gathered her mantle about her. She ordered the doorman to open the door, and he did so reluctantly, pressing her to carry a torch. But Bronwen pushed past him and fled into the darkness.

Dashing down the steep, pebbled hill toward the beach, she felt the frozen ground give way to sand. She threw off her veil and circlet and kicked away her shoes.

Racing alongside the pounding surf, she felt hot tears of anger and shame well up and stream down her cheeks. With no concern for her safety, Bronwen ran and ran—her long braids streaming behind her, falling loose, drifting like a tattered black flag.

Blinded with weeping, she did not see the dark form that sprang up in her path and stopped dead her headlong sprint. Bronwen shrieked in surprise and fear as iron arms pinned her, and a heavy cloak threatened to suffocate her.

"Release me!" she cried. "Guard! Guard, help me."

"Hush, my lady." A deep voice emanated from the darkness. "I mean you no harm. What demon drives you to run through the night without fear for your safety?"

"Release me, villain! I am the daughter—"

"I shall hold you until you calm yourself. We had heard there were witches in Amounderness, but I had not thought to meet one so openly."

Still held tight in the man's arms, Bronwen drew back and peered up at the hooded figure. "You! You are the man who spied on our feast. Release me at once, or I shall call the guard upon you."

The man chuckled at this and turned toward his companions, who stood in a group nearby. Bronwen caught hold of the back of his hood and jerked it down to reveal a head of glossy raven curls. But the man's face was shrouded in darkness yet, and as he looked at her, she could not read his expression.

"So you are the blessed bride-to-be." He returned the hood to his head. "Your father has paired you with an interesting choice."

Relieved that her captor did not appear to be a highwayman, she pushed away from him and sagged onto the wet sand. "Please leave me here alone. I need peace to think. Go on your way."

The tall stranger shrugged off his outer mantle and wrapped it around her shoulders. "Why did your father betroth you thus to the aged Viking?" he asked.

"For one purported to be a spy, you know precious little about Amounderness. But I shall tell you, as it is all common knowledge."

She pulled the cloak tightly about her, reveling in its warmth. "This land, known as Amounderness, once was Briton territory. Olaf Lothbrok, my betrothed, came here as a youth when the Viking invasions had nearly subsided. He took the lands directly to the south of Rossall Hall from their Briton lord. Then, of course, the Normans came, and Amounderness was pillaged by William the Conqueror's army."

The man squatted on the sand beside Bronwen. He listened with obvious interest as she continued. "When William took an account of Amounderness in his Domesday Book, he recorded no remaining lords and few people at all. But he did not know the Britons. Slowly we crept out of hiding and returned to our halls. My father's family reoccupied Rossall Hall. And there we live, as we should, watching over our serfs as they fish and grow their meager crops. Indeed, there is not much here for the greedy Normans to want, if they are the ones for whom you spy."

Unwilling to continue speaking when her heart was so heavy, Bronwen stood and turned toward the sea. The traveler rose beside her and touched her arm. "Olaf Lothbrok's lands—together with your father's—will reunite most of Amounderness under the rule of the son you are beholden to bear. A clever plan. Your sister's future husband holds the rest of the adjoining lands, I understand."

"You've done your work, sir. Your lord will be pleased. Who is he—some land-hungry Scottish baron? Or have you forgotten that King Stephen gave Amounderness to the Scots, as a trade for their support in his war with Matilda? I certainly hope your lord is not a Norman. He would be so disappointed to learn he has no legal rights here. Now, if you will excuse me?"

Bronwen turned and began walking back along the beach toward Rossall Hall. She felt better for her run, and somehow her father's plan did not seem so far-fetched anymore. Distant lights twinkled through the fog that was rolling in from the west, and she suddenly realized what a long way she had come.

"My lady," the man's voice called out behind her.

Bronwen kept walking, unwilling to face again the one who had seen her in her humiliation. She didn't care what he reported to his master.

"My lady, you have quite a walk ahead of you." The traveler strode forward to join her. "I shall accompany you to your destination."

"You leave me no choice, I see."

"I am not one to compromise myself, dear lady. I follow the path God has set before me and none other."

"And just who are you?"

"I am called Jacques."

"French. A Norman, as I had suspected."

The man chuckled. "Not nearly as Norman as you are Briton."

As they approached the fortress, Bronwen could see that the guests had not yet begun to disperse. Perhaps no one had missed her, and she could slip quietly into bed beside Gildan.

She turned to go, but he took her arm and studied her face in the moonlight. Then, gently, he drew her into the folds of his hooded cloak. "Perhaps the bride would like the memory of a younger man's embrace to warm her," he whispered.

Astonished, Bronwen attempted to remove his arms from around her waist. But she could not escape his lips as they found her own. The kiss was soft and warm, melting away her resistance like the sun upon the snow. Before she had time to react, he was striding back down the beach.

Bronwen stood stunned for a moment, clutching his woolen mantle about her. Suddenly she cried out, "Wait, Jacques! Your mantle!"

The dark one turned to her. "Keep it for now," he shouted into the wind. "I shall ask for it when we meet again."

* * * * *

Don't miss this deeply moving story,
THE BRITON,
available February 2008
from the new Love Inspired Historical line.

And also look for
HOMESPUN BRIDE
by Jillian Hart,
where a Montana woman discovers that love
is the greatest blessing of all.

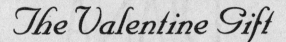

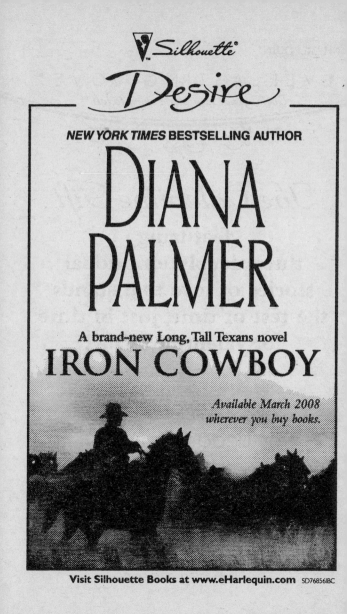

Silhouette® Desire

NEW YORK TIMES BESTSELLING AUTHOR

DIANA PALMER

A brand-new Long, Tall Texans novel

IRON COWBOY

*Available March 2008
wherever you buy books.*

The second book in the deliciously passionate
Heart trilogy by *New York Times* bestselling author

KAT MARTIN

As a viscount's daughter, vivacious Coralee Whitmore
is perfectly placed to write about London's elite in the
outspoken ladies' gazette *Heart to Heart*. But beneath her
fashionable exterior beats the heart of a serious journalist.

So when her sister's death is dismissed as suicide, Corrie vows
to uncover the truth, suspecting that the notorious Earl of
Tremaine was Laurel's lover and the father of her illegitimate
child. But Corrie finds the earl is not all he seems…nor is
she immune to his charms, however much she despises his
caddish ways.

"The first of [a] new series,
Heart of Honor is a grand
way for the author to begin…
Kat Martin has penned
another memorable tale."
—*Historical Romance Writers*

Heart of Fire

*Available the first week of January 2008
wherever paperbacks are sold!*

www.MIRABooks.com

MKM2452

REQUEST YOUR FREE BOOKS!
2 FREE NOVELS PLUS 2
FREE GIFTS!

From the Heart, For the Heart

YES! Please send me 2 FREE Harlequin Romance® novels and my 2 FREE gifts. After receiving them, if I don't wish to receive any more books, I can return the shipping statement marked "cancel." If I don't cancel, I will receive 4 brand-new novels every month and be billed just $3.57 per book in the U.S., or $4.05 per book in Canada, plus 25¢ shipping and handling per book and applicable taxes, if any*. That's a savings of over 15% off the cover price! I understand that accepting the 2 free books and gifts places me under no obligation to buy anything. I can always return a shipment and cancel at any time. Even if I never buy another book from Harlequin, the two free books and gifts are mine to keep forever.

114 HDN EEV7 314 HDN EEWK

Name	(PLEASE PRINT)	
Address		Apt.
City	State/Prov.	Zip/Postal Code

Signature (if under 18, a parent or guardian must sign)

Mail to the Harlequin Reader Service®:
IN U.S.A.: P.O. Box 1867, Buffalo, NY 14240-1867
IN CANADA: P.O. Box 609, Fort Erie, Ontario L2A 5X3

Not valid to current Harlequin Romance subscribers.

Want to try two free books from another line?
Call 1-800-873-8635 or visit www.morefreebooks.com.

* Terms and prices subject to change without notice. NY residents add applicable sales tax. Canadian residents will be charged applicable provincial taxes and GST. This offer is limited to one order per household. All orders subject to approval. Credit or debit balances in a customer's account(s) may be offset by any other outstanding balance owed by or to the customer. Please allow 4 to 6 weeks for delivery.

Your Privacy: Harlequin is committed to protecting your privacy. Our Privacy Policy is available online at www.eHarlequin.com or upon request from the Reader Service. From time to time we make our lists of customers available to reputable firms who may have a product or service of interest to you. If you would prefer we not share your name and address, please check here. ☐

HR07

HARLEQUIN *Super Romance*

Texas Hold 'Em

When it comes to love, the stakes are high

Sixteen years ago, Luke Chisum dated
Becky Parker on a dare...before going
on to break her heart. Now the former
River Bluff daredevil is back, rekindling
desire and tempting Becky to pick up
where they left off. But this time she has
to resist or Luke could discover the secret
she's kept locked away all these years....

Look for

TEXAS BLUFF

by Linda Warren

#1470

*Available February 2008
wherever you buy books.*